"There's nothing between us, Mr. Doukas."

A voice in her head told her she was careless. Reckless. Asking for trouble.

"Isn't there? Are you absolutely sure, Cora? Because it feels to me as if we share...something."

He lifted his hand, hard fingers spreading over her jaw, his thumb a mere heartbeat from her mouth.

She struggled to keep her voice even. Admitting he was right would be a fatal error. "Sorry, Mr. Doukas. You must be imagining it."

His nostrils flared on an indrawn breath and something flashed across his features. It didn't look like anger.

"Maybe you're right. After all, what could we have in common?"

Cora didn't move. She couldn't, because while her brain told her to leave, every cell in her body screamed that this was exactly where she wanted to be.

"Unless, of course, it's this."

His head swooped down to hers and her lips parted on a silent sigh of relief.

Growing up near the beach, **Annie West** spent lots of time observing tall, burnished lifeguards—early research! Now she spends her days fantasizing about gorgeous men and their love lives. Annie has been a reader all her life. She also loves travel, long walks, good company and great food. You can contact her at annie@annie-west.com or via PO Box 1041, Warners Bay, NSW 2282, Australia.

Books by Annie West

Harlequin Presents

Demanding His Desert Queen
Contracted to Her Greek Enemy
Claiming His Out-of-Bounds Bride
The Sheikh's Marriage Proclamation
Pregnant with His Majesty's Heir

Secret Heirs of Billionaires

Sheikh's Royal Baby Revelation

Sovereigns and Scandals

Revelations of a Secret Princess
The King's Bride by Arrangement

Visit the Author Profile page
at Harlequin.com for more titles.

Annie West

A CONSEQUENCE MADE IN GREECE

HARLEQUIN®
PRESENTS®

Recycling programs
for this product may
not exist in your area.

ISBN-13: 978-1-335-56795-6

A Consequence Made in Greece

Copyright © 2021 by Annie West

This edition published by arrangement with Harlequin Books S.A.

For questions and comments about the quality of this book,
please contact us at CustomerService@Harlequin.com.

Harlequin Enterprises ULC
22 Adelaide St. West, 40th Floor
Toronto, Ontario M5H 4E3, Canada
www.Harlequin.com

Printed in U.S.A.

A CONSEQUENCE MADE
IN GREECE

Once again, with feeling, thank you to
Abby Green, Anna Campbell and Efthalia Pegios,
for your help when I needed it.

PROLOGUE

'ARE YOU SURE you don't want to join me?'

Strato slitted his eyes against the sun, taking in the topless woman in his superyacht's swimming pool. Her breasts bobbed in the water but her blonde hair was dry and perfectly styled.

'No. You carry on.'

If he wanted to swim he'd dive off the boat. The waters in this part of western Greece were like crystal. And when Strato swam it was a workout, not a loll in a pool he could traverse in six strokes.

And if he wanted a woman...

That was the problem. He didn't want this woman.

Four days had been ample to remind him he didn't like mindless chatter. That celebrity gossip was no match for an intellectually stimulating discussion or a sense of humour.

And that manufactured passion was no substitute for the real thing. She was enthusiastic, or able to feign enthusiasm, yet there was something lacking.

Strato frowned. There was always something lacking.

The problem, he realised with sudden insight, was with *him*, not her.

He'd avoided deep attachments and emotional relationships since he was old enough to understand their inherent danger. He'd spent his adult life with women content to abide by those restrictions. Ones who enjoyed a good time and a good party. Yet he grew increasingly restless and dissatisfied.

That accounted for his spur of the moment decision to invite Liv and her friend aboard. But instead of enjoying their company, he increasingly avoided them. At least previous lovers had been engaging and there'd been mutual respect and interest.

She pouted, tilting her head coquettishly. 'If you don't want to swim, I could give you a massage.'

Strato shivered. What he wanted was to be left alone. He didn't want bony fingers kneading his shoulders as a prelude to sex that would leave him feeling even emptier than before. If he needed a massage his sports masseur/personal trainer was aboard.

'Perhaps you'd prefer something else?' a throaty voice purred. Strato turned to see his other guest emerge from indoors. She moved sinuously, hips forward and shoulders back, showing off her lean model's body.

Her long hair swung around her shoulders as she watched him from the corner of her eye. Beneath the translucent jewelled caftan she was naked. Her lips curved in a smile that was half invitation, half hungry.

Strato knew her real hunger was reserved for his wealth.

He suppressed a sigh. He was being unfair. He'd got what he asked for. Restlessness had impaired his judgement. It had been his mistake inviting Liv and Lene on this trip, and not just because he'd overestimated their appeal.

He'd specified fun, sex, luxury and no strings, all temporary. But it was clear they thought the term *temporary* was negotiable, already blatantly hinting about longer-term relationships.

Strato couldn't allow them to harbour hopes about permanency. The very thought made his nape prickle.

'Maybe you'd like to join the pair of us?' Lene pulled off her dress with a flourish to reveal her elegant body, then dropped the fabric, stepping into the shallow end of the pool. She beckoned her friend. 'Maybe you'd like to watch me and Liv together and then join in?'

She reached out and stroked her friend's bare flesh from shoulder to thigh.

Two pairs of assessing eyes fixed on Strato. He felt the weight of their calculation. They weren't motivated by desire. Except the desire to please him so he'd keep them in luxury and shower them with expensive trinkets. Or maybe, in a moment of weakness, decide to make one his long-term lover.

Strato smiled and took off his sunglasses. Instantly two smiles, gleaming and perfect, answered as the women moved closer together.

What they didn't know was that his expression hid a surge of disgust. Self-disgust at that.

Had he really thought a cruise with these two would be amusing?

Amusement was the last thing he felt. There was a metallic taste in his mouth and his flesh tightened as distaste stirred.

He'd known what they were. As they'd known what he was. Notorious for his wealth, low boredom threshold and refusal to be caught by any woman.

'Thanks for the invitation, ladies.' He rose and their gazes raked his body.

Okay, maybe he did them an injustice. Their interest in his body wasn't totally manufactured. But that didn't alter the essentials. This wasn't working.

'My apologies, but something has come up unexpectedly.'

He gestured towards the study he'd left minutes before. Let them think he'd received news that required his attention. That would afford them some dignity when he gave them their marching orders.

'Do carry on and enjoy yourselves. But I'm afraid I have to change my plans and regrettably you'll need to return to Athens today.' He paused for that to sink in. 'My helicopter will take you back at sunset, or earlier if you prefer. From there a chauffeur will take you wherever you like.' He nodded. 'Thank you both for your company. It's been memorable.'

He turned and walked across the deck, tuning out the sound of gasps.

His efficient secretary appeared from inside as Strato reached the side of the boat. As ever he was there just when he was needed. 'Fix it please, Manoli. And a suitable gift for each of them.'

Strato stood for a moment, looking across the water to the small island a couple of kilometres away. He breathed deep, drawing in the fresh, salt-tanged air as an antidote to the unpleasant taste on his tongue. Then he executed a perfect dive into the green depths and began swimming.

CHAPTER ONE

STRATO CROSSED THE soft white sand of a tiny beach, heading for a cluster of trees. The swim had made his blood pump and with it had come a possible solution to a business problem that had kept him awake into the night.

It suited him to concentrate on that, rather than the error he'd made inviting Lene and Liv aboard.

He dropped to the sand where an overhanging branch provided shade and stretched out, telling himself to focus on the difficulty his Asian headquarters had raised.

Sometime later a pulsing noise made him look up. There was his chopper, rising from the yacht's helipad. His guests must have decided to head back to the city straight away, to seek out some new sponsor as soon as possible.

Strato's mouth twisted. His lapse of judgement with that pair had left him feeling strangely...diminished. He frowned over the sensation.

Could it be that his deliberate choice of shallow, un-demanding relationships was making him shallow too?

But he could see no way to avoid that. He didn't want people trying to get close. Yet most of the women who were happy with short, physical relationships didn't really engage his interest any more.

Plus, increasingly, they took his warning that he didn't do relationships as an invitation to try. They didn't understand that Strato Doukas had no hidden soft spot. No secret urge for a spouse or family.

His pool of shade turned suddenly icy.

There'd be no wife or family for him.

He tasted bile at the thought. The lessons of his childhood would never be forgotten. His father had seen to that.

Ruthlessly he thrust aside the tainted memories. Far better to focus on work, one of his antidotes to a past best forgotten.

But before he could concentrate on his Asian business issue, he caught sight of a small boat, white with a painted trim of aqua and red, puttering towards the island.

Strato sighed. He wanted solitude, not a bunch of day trippers. But as he squinted into the sunlight he saw just one figure, wearing a wide straw hat and bulky shirt.

The little vessel approached till it was off the rocky tip at the end of the beach. A picnicker? It had better not be a paparazzo.

The intruder whipped off the wide hat and Strato stared. A she. With dark hair almost to her waist. His eyebrows rose. Hair like that wasn't something you saw every day.

Nevertheless, he must focus on this logistics problem…

With one swift movement the big shirt came off to reveal a figure that actually snared his breath.

Just as you didn't see hair like that often, nor did you see bodies like that, at least in his social circles.

She twisted and bent to stow the hat and shirt and he registered her suppleness—always a plus—as well as her spectacular curves. The newcomer had an hour-glass figure. The sort that, sadly, seemed to have gone out of fashion.

After his slim-to-the-bone guests this week, the ripe swells and tantalising dips of this woman's figure drew his gaze like a beacon. He watched as she wriggled her hips, pushing down a pair of baggy shorts to re-veal more lush curves. Even the dowdy dark one-piece swimsuit didn't detract for it fitted like a second skin.

His lips curved. Perhaps he wouldn't mind meeting a picnicker after all.

Yet instead of coming ashore, she put on a mask and snorkel and lowered herself off the far side of the boat, heading into deeper water. For five minutes he watched, curious about the back-and-forth pattern of her swim.

Whoever she was, she was in little danger of drown-ing. Those long legs kicked powerfully and she moved with grace and precision. But eventually she swam to the headland and past it, out of sight.

Probably just as well. He'd come here to be alone. The last thing he needed was another woman distract-ing him. He stretched and rolled over, turning away from the water.

Cora jammed the hat more firmly on her head as she picked her way across the rocks, eyes on the ground. Only when she reached the sugar-fine sand did she look towards the shady grove she'd taken to using for her lunch break.

And discovered she wasn't alone.

A figure lay in the deep shade.

No one else came to this tiny islet, except in the height of the summer season when occasional day trippers from the main island might stop. She turned to survey the water. The only boat in sight, apart from the little wooden one she'd borrowed from her father, was a huge, sleek cruiser in the distance. The sort that looked more at home in Piraeus or the Bahamas than in this forgotten corner of Greece.

Cora frowned, noticing the single set of footprints emerging from the sea.

People who cruised the world in those swanky big yachts didn't swim four kilometres for fun. Had his boat sunk? He couldn't have come ashore in last night's storm. The footprints were too fresh.

Frowning, she headed up the beach. She hoped he wasn't injured.

Her stride slowed then stopped as she got closer. A man lay on his side, his back to her.

He was naked. The same dark olive colour from his wide, straight shoulders, down the curve of his tapering back to tightly rounded buttocks and long, hairy legs.

Cora swallowed. Surprise dried her mouth and caught her lungs. She felt her eyes widen.

This man was big, she realised. Really big, with long limbs and a toned, fit body.

She was used to fit, athletic men, given her work. Yet she didn't think she'd ever seen one like this.

Would he look as spectacular from the front?

A tiny breeze riffled his dark hair but he didn't move. Her eyes strayed to a discoloured area spreading from the shoulder he lay on, up towards his shoulder blade.

Her frown deepened. An injury? Not blood, surely?

Dropping her canvas holdall, she rushed up to him, the tang of fear on her tongue. Was he breathing?

She bent and a hiss escaped her. Shock and relief. Not blood. That wasn't a recent injury. It was old scar tissue. A burn or—

Muscles rippled under dark gold skin and he rolled over, his shoulder sliding against her ankle, making her jump back.

Spectacular was the word. She had an impression of streamlined power, of formidable energy before she forced her attention up. Yet that momentary survey of his naked form had her heart thudding. Spectacular was definitely the word. Spectacular all over.

Cora swallowed hard and focused on his face. A broad brow. Severe, straight black eyebrows and beneath them slitted green eyes.

Poseidon. That was who he looked like.

Every Greek had seen likenesses of the mighty sea god, the personification of male strength and beauty. Surely if the old stories of gods appearing to mortals held any truth, Poseidon would have eyes like that. Stormy. Assessing. The colour of the sea she'd just swum in.

Cora's mouth dried. 'You're alive.'

'You were expecting a corpse?'

The fine hairs on Cora's arms rose and something unfamiliar breathed into being. As if that deep, amused voice woke something dormant within her.

She stiffened and took another half-step back.

'I wasn't sure what to think.' Maybe she'd had too much sun. When she met that probing green gaze her vision seemed to blur at the edges.

Cora broke eye contact and looked past him, frowning.

'You've got no towel, no clothes.' Amazing how tough it was not to let her gaze dip to his lower body. One quick look had already revealed he was built on the same monumental scale all over. Heat rose to her face.

Those straight eyebrows arched. 'Is there some rule that says I must have them with me at all times?'

'I wondered if you'd had an accident.'

'Is that why you were bending over me? To give me mouth to mouth?'

Her gaze dropped, past a long, straight nose to his smiling mouth. His mouth was beautifully formed, almost too beautiful for a man. Except that the rest of his features, from his solidly carved jaw to the high-cut planes of his cheeks, were so overtly masculine. A deep groove bisected one cheek where his wryly amused smile rose more on one side than the other.

There was no way you could call it a dimple.

A dimple implied something cute and appealing.

This face, this smile, was sardonic, not cute. As for appealing… Her thrumming pulse was proof of that.

But Cora was no fool. He might be incredibly charismatic, with that sexy, quintessentially masculine body. But there was a sharpness about him she didn't like.

As any Greek who knew their myths could tell you, the ancient gods weren't kind, caring creatures. They were dangerous.

This man was too. Every feminine instinct sensed danger. The danger not of violence but of primal awareness between male and female.

It showed in the sharp speculation belying that ostensibly lazy stare. In the way his gaze flickered to the damp patches where her breasts pressed against the worn denim shirt. And in the way that smile broadened into something like interest as he saw her noticing.

And above all in the fact he didn't make a move to cover his nakedness, just lay there, as if inviting her to appreciate his assets.

'Right. Well, if you're okay, I'll go.' This might be the only deeply shaded spot on the tiny island and she might be long overdue her lunch but—

'How do you know I'm okay? You haven't checked my pulse.'

Strato surveyed his Nereid with curiosity and a surprisingly sharp jab of pleasure. For she was definitely a Nereid, a sea nymph.

She'd been the one snorkelling. Her hair hung in long slick locks and there were crease marks on her face from her goggles. Besides, even the frumpy shirt and long baggy shorts couldn't hide her phenomenal body.

But then he'd had the advantage of seeing her luscious body in all its glory and he had an excellent memory.

Her eyebrows pinched and wide golden-brown eyes met his with a mix of impatience and suspicion that was as obvious as it was novel. Women didn't usually look at him that way.

Usually they looked eager.

He lifted a hand to his forehead and saw her attention drop to his biceps. Suspicion narrowed her eyes.

Okay, it was an obvious move, drawing attention to his muscles. But he'd seen the way those eyes had widened as she'd looked him over, dwelling for a second on his penis. He understood that look. Had seen it so often from so many women over the years. Annoyance had stirred at her dismissal. She'd actually been turning away when his words stopped her.

This woman was definitely different. After that first appreciative stare she'd kept her attention on his face.

Strato found that intriguing. Almost disappointing.

He shouldn't want female attention. He'd just sent away the two women who'd joined him for sun and sex.

Either he was so supremely shallow that he couldn't stand being ignored by a lovely woman. Or so world-weary a hint of novelty grabbed his attention—and other parts, making them stir with interest. Neither said much for his character.

Ruefully he decided he might be both. Though no one else would dare voice such an assessment. Not when Strato Doukas commanded billions.

He added cynical to the list.

'Are you all right? Did you hurt your head?'

Strato realised his palm covered his forehead and it might look as if he had a headache.

For a nanosecond he contemplated lying. But he preferred the truth, even when it was brutal. Better the truth than hiding from it. He knew first-hand how perilous it could be, not facing facts head-on.

His mouth tightened and in response a frown gathered on her brow.

To his amazement Strato felt warmth lick behind his ribs. Warmth that had nothing to do with sexual interest but with the fact this woman he didn't know was genuinely worried about him.

It was bizarre.

He paid a host of staff extremely well to cater to his every need. He didn't need a stranger's worry. Yet her words stirred something deep inside that he hadn't experienced in a long time.

Raking his fingers through his hair, he gave her a deliberately languid smile, refusing to dwell on his instinctive reaction to her simple kindness. That felt too much like weakness. 'No, I'm not injured. Do I look it?'

Satisfaction scudded through him as he watched her swallow, as if fighting her instinctive response. Because she liked what she saw?

Shallow, Doukas. Definitely shallow.

But better than dwelling on his response to her concern.

'Good. I'm glad you're okay.' Her voice had a throaty edge that rippled across his libido.

She didn't look glad. She looked strung too tight. Strato liked that. He also liked the way her nipples stood erect against her shabby shirt, making him wonder if those plump breasts would feel as spectacular in his hands as they looked.

But shallow though he might be, he was also ruthlessly honest with himself. Which left him thinking about why her interest pleased him. Because it counteracted that momentary jab of unexpected connection he felt? Gave him something to concentrate on other than the emptiness growing inside?

He heard himself saying as she made to turn away, 'I don't suppose you have anything to drink, do you? I'm parched.'

She stilled. 'You don't have any water? How long have you been here?'

He shrugged. 'Hours, I suppose.'

'You suppose? Don't you know? Do you have *any* supplies with you?'

Her voice married concern with a scolding edge and Strato found himself imagining her dressed as a buttoned-up school mistress. It wasn't a fantasy that had ever appealed before. It didn't last long now. He preferred the prospect of seeing her in her swimsuit again, or naked, than with her figure obscured.

'I don't have anything at all.'

Now he thought about it he *was* thirsty. He should have returned to the yacht, because his staff wouldn't seek him out, knowing he wanted solitude.

Not as clever as you thought, Doukas.

He was rewarded with another frown, more like a scowl this time, and a mutter he didn't catch.

'What are you doing without supplies? It's madness.'

He nodded, fascinated. It had been a lifetime ago that anyone had taken him to task. The last had been his aunt, who'd fretted over him, worrying about him till the end. As if her worry could change the inevitable and turn him into someone different, someone not—

'It may not be high summer yet but you can't afford to get dehydrated. Especially if you're alone here.' His Nereid paused, looking beyond him as if expecting to see someone else emerge over the crest of the small hill. '*Are* you alone?'

'I am. But I'll be picked up at sunset.' That was the standing arrangement with his crew.

Her mouth firmed into a disapproving line as she slid a stained canvas bag from her shoulder. 'That's sheer stupidity. *Anything* could happen in that time.'

His gaze tracked from her wide, kissable mouth, now primed with disapproval, down the slick dark hair dripping around her shoulders and lower, reaching towards her waist. Past bountiful breasts to those horribly baggy shorts that made her hips look over-sized, to toned, glorious legs.

Oh, yes, anything could happen in that time.

'I don't suppose you've got any food in there too? I haven't eaten today.'

CHAPTER TWO

CORA PAUSED IN the act of rifling through her bag, her head lifting at the sound of that oh-so-nonchalant voice.

She didn't trust it. She didn't trust *him* further than she could shove that outrageously spectacular body. She was tall and fit but he looked taller and fitter.

Her gaze slid down across that broad chest with its light smattering of hair. Just dark enough to emphasise his defined pectoral muscles and—

Damn! She dragged her attention back to his face.

It gave nothing away. In fact it was suspiciously blank of expression, which would have made her hackles rise even if she hadn't seen the knowing gleam in those sea-green eyes.

He was laughing at her.

The sensible thing would be to leave him to his amusement. Cora had an inbuilt hatred of being the source of any man's amusement. Once bitten…

But she had a strong sensible streak, as well as too much experience of people coming to grief, especially in and near the sea. People who thought it would be okay to try scuba diving without lessons, or drive jet skis while drunk. Or get so badly sunburnt they needed medical care.

At least Poseidon had enough sense to lie in the shade, and from the bronzed colour of his skin he wasn't going to burn any time soon.

She sucked in a breath, realising her attention had dipped to those wide straight shoulders. And he'd noticed.

She wanted to wipe the smirk off his face. Okay, he might not be overtly smiling but inwardly he was laughing at her expense. Her nape tightened at a flash of memory. Adrian, golden haired and blue eyed. Laughing.

Her nostrils flared as she inhaled deeply.

If her instincts were right, this man and Adrian had a lot in common.

But you don't know for sure. And you can't leave him here without even a drink.

Cora wanted to ask how he came to be here, alone, naked and without provisions, but no doubt it would be some story of a stupid joke by friends. Besides, she suspected any show of curiosity would feed his ego.

She sighed. 'You can have some of my lunch if you like.'

Doris always packed too much food, believing that a *big girl* like Cora needed a lot of fuel. It was true that when she worked in the field, Cora burned up a lot of energy and needed extra calories. Yet she hated being categorised as a *big girl*. Even at twenty-six those words hurt. Just as well motherly Doris had no idea. She'd be upset if she knew.

'That would be excellent. Thank you.' He propped himself up on one elbow and gave her a flashing smile that would have weakened her knees if she wasn't immune to gorgeous, self-centred men.

She shifted her weight in the sand. Okay, maybe there was a little melting of the tendons, but she had this man's measure. Forewarned was forearmed.

As for being the butt of his amusement…

'On one condition.'

Cora almost laughed at the way his dark eyebrows shot up in a look of astonishment that was clearly genuine. It appeared nobody was in the habit of denying Poseidon what he wanted, or setting limits on his games.

Interesting to know. That could explain his aura of casual confidence. But then, people gifted with amazing looks were usually confident.

'What is it?' His eyebrows lowered and eyes slitted so his stare looked full of suspicion.

Cora couldn't prevent her huff of laughter. 'Don't fret. I'm not asking for a share of all your worldly goods.' She gestured at the empty sand around him.

When she met his eyes again he wore a curious expression she couldn't identify.

It struck her she was spending far too much energy puzzling over a stranger she'd never see again.

'I prefer not to eat lunch with a naked stranger. I'd rather you covered up.'

'To preserve your modesty?' His long mouth twitched in a way Cora found too attractive. Until his gaze moved to her damp shirt, where her wet hair and swimsuit made the fabric cling to her breasts. 'I'm afraid I've got nothing to cover myself with.' He paused and she felt the silence with each ponderous beat of her pulse. 'Unless you could spare me some clothing?'

Cora swallowed a smile. Someone should warn him about overplaying his hand. It was obvious he wanted her to strip off her shirt. She hadn't missed those quick glances at her breasts where, to her chagrin, her nipples were tight, hard peaks.

'You don't have hang-ups about wearing a woman's clothes? Some men might feel their manhood compromised.'

'If it's that or starvation, I'll opt for the clothes. My ego's not that fragile.'

She'd bet it wasn't.

This time it wasn't a short huff of laughter but a chuckle that escaped. If he was trying for soulful and half-starved he shouldn't look so strong and able-bodied. She'd never met a less pitiable specimen.

'Okay.' She swung her bag down to the sand between them, noticing from the corner of her vision the way he rose higher on his elbow as if intent on the striptease he expected. Cora straightened and put her hands to the hem of her over-sized shirt. Yes, there it was, a flash of anticipation in that hooded gaze.

For a second longer she hesitated, genuinely this time. Wondering if this was a huge mistake.

She could leave a bottle of water with him or offer him a lift back to the harbourside town on the next island where his friends presumably were.

But she was hungry. Why should she have to leave and eat in the sun because of some thoughtless tourist?

The fact that she enjoyed the verbal sparring between them was another factor. How long since her pulse had raced like that? Since she'd felt anything out of the ordinary?

Besides, she rather liked getting one up on this self-satisfied stranger. It was time someone showed him he couldn't have everything his own way.

So instead of reefing her shirt over her head, she

grabbed her baggy, knee-length shorts and tugged them off with one quick movement.

'There you are.' She bent and retrieved them from the sand, giving them a little shake before tossing them into Poseidon's lap.

His surprise almost made her laugh.

Except it was quickly eclipsed by something that made her bones soften. An eager heat in those narrowed eyes as he surveyed her legs and smiled.

Cora felt that sliding gaze almost like a caress and it banished her momentary sense of victory.

Idiot! She might not have uncovered her body but it seemed this stranger was almost as appreciative of bare legs. His smile morphed from appreciative to hungry, heading towards predatory.

Cora's amusement vanished.

She jammed her fists on her hips, grateful that her shirt covered her to her thighs.

'If you want to share my food we need to get one thing straight. *I'm* not on the menu. Got it? I'm not staying alone here with a man who thinks I'm available for his sexual convenience.'

The vibe she'd got from him wasn't the sort she'd had from men who'd take without asking. She was sure, pretty sure, that for all his smug amusement she wasn't in physical peril. Nevertheless, he needed to understand the ground rules or she'd be back at the boat before he could stop her.

Strato stared up into fiery eyes the colour of his favourite brandy. Heat drilled down his gullet, as if he'd slugged back a double measure. But it wasn't from sexual anticipation. For he read defiance in her expression and something that might have been worry. Or fear.

For the first time he viewed the situation from her perspective. Alone on a deserted island with a man she knew nothing about. A man who was far bigger and stronger than her. Who made no secret of his sexual interest. And no one within shouting distance to help her if she needed it.

It wasn't the fire of carnal attraction surging through him. It felt like shame.

He blinked, digesting the unfamiliar sensation.

Unfamiliar, because his casual flirting was always done with women who were patently eager for his attention. Who knew he wanted sex with no strings. Who knew his reputation for ensuring his partners' pleasure. In that world innuendo was pleasurable foreplay.

Now he was out of his usual environment. His Nereid didn't know she had nothing to fear. She hadn't a clue who he was, or that he'd never hurt any woman.

His mouth tightened as he slammed down impenetrable shutters that locked away ancient memories. He never opened them. Except in his nightmares.

Strato raised his hand in a placating gesture and sat up.

'I'm very sorry. I didn't mean to make you uncomfortable.' He swallowed, surprised to find his throat tight so the words emerged like a growl. 'I didn't think. I was just…'

'Flirting.' She sighed and her shoulders eased down a little.

He'd done that. Made her uncomfortable, not in a sexually aroused way, but because she was nervous.

'You have my word of honour that you are totally safe.'

A muscle in his jaw flexed as he gritted his teeth. How could he have made such a mistake? He'd become so used to the sexual promiscuity of a self-indulgent lifestyle that he took it for the norm.

Clearly his Nereid didn't come from that world.

Was that why he found her fascinating?

No, it was more than that. More even than her sexual allure. He liked that she didn't take any nonsense but said what she thought. Liked her quick thinking and humour, turning the tables on him when she guessed he wanted her to take off her shirt.

She was attracted, he knew that. He guessed she could be enticed into wanting him. But this wasn't the place or time for seduction.

He couldn't recall ever making such a mistake in seducing a woman.

Which shows how easy you've had it, Doukas. You never have to exert yourself.

'If you'd prefer to leave, I won't die of thirst, I promise.' He reached for the shorts she'd thrown at him, ready to pass them back. Stoically he ignored that they were warm from her body.

'No. Keep them. You might be glad of the cover if you're really staying here till sunset.'

Something within him sank. Disappointment? Because a chance-met woman was turning her back on him?

Strato told himself it was a novel experience and, since his life seemed so flat and mundane lately, he should welcome that.

Instead he felt absurdly bereft.

'Thank you. And thank you for coming to check on me. It was decent of you.'

He felt like a kid, reminded of his manners. Yet he doubted this chastened feeling would last.

She shook her head, long tresses sliding around her breasts in a way that made Strato lock his jaw and concentrate on her face.

She wasn't beautiful but there was something about her wide mouth and warm, intelligent eyes that *felt* like beauty. Especially when amusement had danced across her face.

He was used to women with bleached, perfect smiles, pumped-up lips and lots of make-up. When this woman smiled he noticed a couple of her teeth overlapped and as for Botox—she had full lips but he'd swear they were natural.

'Are you really hungry, or did you just say that?'

'Starving. It's my own fault. I only had coffee this morning.'

Strato had only downed a tiny cup of coffee before heading into his office, knowing it was the one place his guests wouldn't follow.

'In that case…' She shrugged. 'We might as well eat. This is the only shade around and I usually have lunch here.'

Pleasure was a punch to his solar plexus. It was on the tip of his tongue to ask if she came here often but it was such a cliché and he'd promised not to play flirtatious games. Instead he simply grinned his approval.

Her response was instantaneous. Her eyes flared with a heat that reminded him of warmed cognac. Her breasts rose on a sharp breath that would have stoked his ego if he weren't used to female admiration.

Strato pretended not to notice. He'd concentrate instead on the simple pleasure of lunch by the sea with a fascinating companion.

Even so, he knew that in the right circumstances, he could find another sort of pleasure with this woman. But it wouldn't be simple. And he only did simple, didn't he?

Or were his tastes changing?

Was that why he'd been so restless lately? And why she appealed so much?

'Thank you for trusting me,' he murmured. 'It's generous of you. Now, do you want to turn around while I dress?'

Remarkably for a woman who'd stood up to him as no one else did and who berated him for his sexually charged interactions, rosy colour swept into her cheeks.

That blush intrigued. She was no wilting violet, scared to face a man. Yet she was a strange mix of confidence and reserve. He couldn't recall the last time he'd seen a woman blush.

Strato hadn't met anyone like her.

'Good idea. I'll see what Doris packed for lunch.' She turned, ostentatiously busying herself with her canvas bag.

Damp cotton bunched in Strato's hands. He'd originally hoped she'd strip off her shirt but he couldn't complain about the view.

Her tanned legs would feature in his dreams. They were shapely and long. Long enough that he wouldn't have to bend double to kiss her. Strong too, given all the swimming she'd done. Strong enough to wrap around him and grip hard as he drove deep into her luscious warmth.

Nostrils flaring, he shook the sand from the shorts with a snap and put them on.

If only the press could see you now, Doukas.

Billionaire sets new fashion trend! It puts a whole new spin on wanting to get into her pants.

He huffed out a silent laugh.

The shorts were ancient, faded and a terrible fit. But they were warm from her body and he had to take a few moments to battle his stirring erection as he imagined her naked and willing against him. It was an image his fertile imagination didn't want to relinquish.

Fortunately she didn't notice as she unpacked lunch.

Strato breathed deep and reminded himself he didn't want to scare her off.

He'd promised to behave.

For now.

Later, when she understood he was no threat, it might be intriguing to pursue this sudden attraction.

'Who's Doris?'

Cora looked over her shoulder and her stupid heart gave a shuddery heave then catapulted into a rackety beat.

She'd seen him sprawled naked. How could he look even more mouth-wateringly male wearing daggy old shorts?

Yet somehow the contrast between dark golden skin stretched over honed muscle and shabby, faded cotton made him look even sexier.

Maybe it was the nonchalant way he wore the threadbare shorts. His total lack of concern over his appearance, his casual confidence in his own skin were devastatingly attractive to a woman who'd spent too many years overly conscious of her body shape.

On him, tall and well-built would never be called over-sized. He looked gorgeous.

'Sorry?'

'You mentioned Doris. I wondered who she was.'

'Oh.' Cora dragged her gaze back to the food. 'She's the cook at my father's hotel.'

In fact she was far more.

Cora's mother died when she was eight, and for the next six years it had just been her and her father, till Doris arrived. The newcomer had been good for them both, breathing new life into the place. She'd also taken Cora under her wing, providing a sounding board through the trials of her teen years, even trying to tame her so she didn't become a total tomboy.

Cora's lips twitched. Poor Doris. She was a dear, so loyal and caring. She'd tried her best to turn Cora into a model of housewifely virtues but with limited success.

'You live with your father?'

She caught a flash of curiosity. It wasn't surprising for multiple generations to live together, especially in traditional villages such as her own. Clearly this stranger wasn't from such a background.

Cora glanced out to sea where, in the distance, that massive cruiser was moored. It had come from Athens, Doris reported, after some crew came into harbour for provisions.

'For the moment. He hasn't been well.'

She swallowed, recalling that horrible long-distance call. The news her father had suffered a heart attack. The terrible helplessness of being more than a continent away and unable to be with him straight away.

'I'm sorry to hear that.'

She shrugged and spread the packets of food between them. 'He's improved a lot. He's doing better.'

Or he would be if he weren't so stressed about the hotel. The economic downturn had hit hard, just after he'd taken out a huge loan, investing in major improvements that he'd thought would set the business up for long-term profit. Now they faced a particularly poor tourist season, with bookings down and no idea how they'd meet the repayments.

Naturally Cora had stayed to help.

'I'm glad he's okay.' The stranger paused and Cora sensed his scrutiny. To her relief he turned his attention to the food. 'Your Doris has provided a feast.'

'She doesn't do things by halves.' Cora smiled and broke a large piece of cheese and spinach pie apart, passing him half. 'She even makes her own filo pastry.'

He took a bite and Cora watched him pause, eyes widening then narrowing to unreadable slits as he slowly savoured it. He took another, bigger bite.

Doris would approve of him. She liked anyone who appreciated her cooking. Cora turned her attention back to the food though, strangely uncomfortable watching his obvious enjoyment. His gusto made her wonder if he attacked other physical pleasures with the same enthusiasm.

Absurdly she felt that phantom brush of heat in her cheeks again. Because once more her thoughts turned carnal.

'That's real home cooking,' he said, what sounded like genuine emotion drawing Cora's curiosity. It was more than simple appreciation. 'I haven't tasted food like this for years.'

Yet he wasn't starved. That imposing body was impressive.

'No one cooks like that for you?' She refused to ask if he had a wife. If he did she pitied the woman, for this man had the unmistakable air of someone committed to pleasure without concern for others.

'Not since I was young.' He took another bite with strong, white teeth and Cora watched, mesmerised, the rhythmic action of his jaw and the way his throat muscles worked as he swallowed.

She unscrewed a bottle of water and took a swig.

'May I?' He nodded to the bottle and she passed it, watching him put it to his lips.

Glittering eyes surveyed her over the raised bottle and she turned away, dismayed at her body's reaction. Because he'd put his mouth where hers had been. Which made her think of his mouth on hers. Which made her breasts tighten and heat stir low in her pelvis.

This was *so* not her. Maybe she was the one who'd had a touch too much sun. She certainly wasn't responding to Poseidon as she normally did to men.

With a huff of annoyance she shoved salad and olives towards him, then the bread. Normally Cora would have eaten ravenously after all her exertions. Now her appetite waned.

Sharing lunch with this man had been a mistake. He mightn't be physically dangerous but he disturbed her in ways no man had since Adrian. And even with Adrian—

'You're not eating.'

She looked up to find him watching her. For an instant everything inside sparked to alert, then his gaze slid away towards the beach as if appreciating the view and she relaxed.

Cora frowned. A single look did that? Did he realise? Was that why he turned away?

Slowly she reached for an orange. 'I suspect your need is greater than mine.'

Which was nonsense. She'd been hungry before. Frowning, she concentrated on peeling the fruit, inhaling the citrus tang and popping a juicy segment into her mouth.

Silence lengthened as they ate. Gradually Cora felt her shoulders lower, her tight muscles easing.

Someone seeing them would think the atmosphere companionable as they concentrated on the view.

Yet Cora was totally aware of the man beside her. The reach of his long arm as he explored the goodies Doris had provided. The easy shift and stretch of his long body as he got more comfortable on the sand.

Her own body kept leaning closer, till she realised what she was doing and pulled back.

Determined, Cora concentrated on her orange and thinking of something else.

It had been a tough morning with that reminder from the bank sending her father into something like panic.

Usually her trips to this tiny island helped her deal with the stress over her father and the hotel, which she feared they'd lose. Today even the sea, which always brought solace, failed her.

Because more than half her mind was on Poseidon, happily devouring her food, rather than on devising some new strategy to save her dad from bankruptcy.

Abruptly she came to a decision. Her earlier instincts had been right. This was a mistake.

Licking the sticky juice from her fingers, she reached for the water bottle and poured some over her palms. Then she rose. 'I have to go.'

'You're leaving?'

She saw surprise on Poseidon's honed features. Genuine surprise, not feigned.

Cora felt satisfaction unfurl. Given his penchant for flirting and the way he guarded his thoughts, it felt like a victory to see his astonished look.

He probably wasn't used to women leaving till he was finished with them.

She drew a shaky breath and told herself that didn't apply to her because she'd never let him start with her. There'd be no casual passion with a stranger. Not for her.

'It's time.' She hesitated then made the offer that any decent person would. 'Can I give you a lift?'

His narrowed eyes caught hers and she felt a frisson of awareness skid down her spine and curl into her belly. She swallowed. Given her history she'd prided herself on her defences against predatory men. This man made a mockery of those. With just a look!

'Thank you, no. I'm fine.' His hand dropped to those ancient shorts. 'You'll want these back.'

'No!' Did her voice sound strangled? 'Thanks, but I don't want them.'

Even if she could wear them with half the panache he did, she'd rather not see them again. They'd remind her of today's madness. That sudden surging hunger. For a complete stranger!

For a second longer Cora looked at him. Trying to imprint his image in her memory? Abruptly she turned away.

* * *

Strato watched her cross the beach, the loose sand turning each step into an undulating sway of curvaceous hips that dried his mouth. He groped for the water bottle and gulped.

Now she was on firm sand and her walk became an athletic stride, the movement of her long, gilded legs mesmerising.

Oh, yes, he'd dream about those legs.

He took another gulp. But his dry throat had nothing to do with the need for water.

It was all down to *her*.

When was the last time a woman walked out on him?

He understood that she was wary of a complete stranger. So he'd masked his thoughts and projected an aura of calm.

It had worked. They'd sat companionably. Long enough for him to become addicted to the sight of her eating that damned orange. He'd swear she didn't realise how the sight of her pink tongue, swiping up drips of juice, teased him. Or how he'd watched her licking her fingers and wished she'd lick him instead.

His frown became a scowl.

Strato had a reputation as a playboy but the gaps between lovers grew longer and even he had never dumped a woman or, in today's case, two, and instantly pursued another! He didn't understand it.

There was something about this woman that called to him.

Sexual allure, obviously.

But more too. Character. That was it. Feistiness melded with…decency. Her concern for him had been real, even through her annoyance. That concern had made him feel things he hadn't experienced in a long time.

That didn't say much for the people he mixed with, did it?

Even the lunch she'd shared had stirred unfamiliar yearnings. That cheese pie reminded him of his mother's. A tantalising flavour he hadn't tasted since he was eight. It had been like biting into sunshine and rare memories of happiness. No wonder he felt unsettled.

His eyes narrowed as his Nereid disappeared around the point without a backward glance. She had no interest in prolonging their acquaintance.

Or did she know that by leaving she'd pique his interest?

Whatever the reasons, this woman fascinated him, far more than anyone he could recall.

Strato reached for the segment of orange she'd left. He bit into it, tasting the bright sunburst of sweet, tart citrus. His tongue tingled as he sucked up the juice.

Strato closed his eyes and imagined it wasn't an orange he was feasting on but her.

The question was, would he give in to temptation?

CHAPTER THREE

CORA WAS WIPING down outdoor tables on the vine-shaded terrace when she heard a boat.

It wasn't unusual to hear motors early in the morning as the fishing boats returned. Yet this motor approached the hotel, not the harbour further around the bay.

She shaded her eyes. On the water's dancing gold and silver dazzle she saw it approach. Not a traditional fishing boat but something sleek and modern.

They weren't expecting guests today, sadly. Besides, this boat was too small to have come from the mainland. Cora scanned the bay and noticed the luxury motor yacht she'd seen yesterday, now anchored off the point. If someone was coming ashore for supplies, surely they'd head to the harbourside shops?

The engine stopped and the boat kissed the end of the hotel's jetty. Someone slung out a rope, mooring it with the ease of long practice.

She moved to the next table. Yet instead of cleaning it, she watched the man walk down the jetty.

The low sun was directly behind him and she had an impression of height and athleticism, and wide, straight shoulders. He didn't hurry but his long stride covered the distance in no time.

Cora's nape tightened and the cloth crumpled in her hand as she watched that easy, confident walk. More saunter than stride.

She didn't recognise his gait, yet premonition stirred like a strong current in still waters. Some primal sense told her—

He stepped into the shade of the tamarisk trees edging the terrace and Cora's chest grabbed.

Poseidon.

The amused, intriguing, dangerous man from yesterday.

Her eyes ate him up. From the dark hair swept back off his high forehead to the chiselled male beauty and carved arrogance of his face. He wore reflective sunglasses and she wondered if behind them he was smiling again.

One sweeping glance told her he looked almost as good dressed as he did naked. He wore designer loafers, a white short-sleeved shirt, and pale trousers that must have been tailored to fit those powerful thighs and long legs.

Instantly Cora regretted her choice of clothes. Old tennis shoes, cut-off denim shorts with uneven, ragged edges and a black T-shirt proclaiming *Biologists Do It in Their Genes*.

He stopped on the terrace, surveying her. Then slowly, so slowly she felt each tiny, incremental change like the stroke of velvet on bare skin, his mouth curved up into a smile that made her pulse throb and her toes curl.

A flourish of something she couldn't name stirred and Cora snatched a desperate breath, schooling her features.

She tilted her chin higher. She'd been right. He was tall, far taller than her. It was unusual for her to have to look up at a man. Unusual and...not unpleasant.

'Good morning. Can I help you?'

Sleek eyebrows lifted and he took his glasses off to reveal eyes the colour of the sea, shimmering with warmth.

'You don't recognise me?' His smile curved even higher on one side, creating an apostrophe of amusement, a tiny groove in the tanned flesh beside his mouth.

It was like an invitation, that tiny curl. Beckoning Cora to reach out and trace it. To respond to the invitation in his eyes.

Remarkably, her fingertips tingled as if she'd done just that. As if she'd brushed them across his face.

Horrified at her vivid imaginings, she reached for the cloth that had dropped to the table.

'Of course. We met yesterday.' Her voice was appallingly husky but she ploughed on. 'So you got picked up from the beach all right.'

He inclined his head, his eyes not leaving hers. 'You were worried about me?'

'I...' Why did her mouth dry under that wickedly arousing gaze and her words stick in her throat? She was twenty-six, not sixteen. 'It was an unusual situation, being left without supplies.'

She'd almost returned yesterday evening to check on him, but her father had felt fretful, worrying about money, and Doris had been out so Cora had been forced to stay here. That was why she'd started her morning chores early, so she had time to take the boat this morning and check the stranger was safe.

'Why are you here?'

'To see you.'

Fervently Cora hoped he couldn't read her delight at his words. She had no interest any more in uber-sexy men. Her dear dad was the only man in her life these days.

Yet excitement throbbed in her accelerating pulse.

'Really?' Willpower kept her voice flat. 'How did you find me?'

He shrugged. 'I knew you must be local.' Then she noticed he held something in his hand. He offered it to her.

'Thank you for the loan.'

Cora's lips twitched as she took the familiar, worn-thin fabric. 'You *ironed* my shorts?'

His smile widened, a long groove appearing in his cheek, and Cora had to focus on taking the clothing rather than melting at the knees.

She'd known attractive men, sexy men, but never one to affect her like this, so devastatingly. Not even Adrian had had this instantaneous impact.

'They've been washed too, but I admit I didn't do it. One of my staff was responsible.'

He had staff? Once more her gaze flickered to that massive yacht. Surely not. He couldn't be the owner. He must have come from elsewhere.

'Well, thank you.' She didn't mention she'd been on the verge of throwing out the tatty shorts.

'Join me in a coffee?'

Cora blinked.

'You do serve coffee here?' He nodded to the small tables and blue-painted, rush-bottomed chairs.

'Of course.' It was before normal opening hours but…

'Then two coffees please. If you'll join me?'

Looking into that confident face, Cora wanted to say she had too much work to spare the time. Any man who made her feel hot and bothered with just a smile should be avoided. It had been a hard-won lesson that she wouldn't forget.

Yet the adventurous Cora she'd stifled so long urged her to agree. The Cora who'd revelled in new experiences, new places and the opportunity to work in the field she loved. The work she'd had to give up while she helped out here.

Lately she'd imagined that Cora had disappeared completely, broken by disappointment, duty and worry. Now, feeling her blood effervesce, she knew better.

Caution vied with pleasure. How long since she'd had a conversation that didn't centre on the hotel, her father's health or their financial woes? At least this man distracted her from reality, even if only fleetingly.

What harm could a coffee do? It was only polite to thank him after he'd made the effort to wash and return her clothes.

Nodding, trying to look brisk and businesslike, she turned away. 'I won't be long.'

Strato subsided onto a chair where he could watch the shadowed doorway through which she'd exited.

Contentment filled him, and a little jiggle of anticipation he hadn't experienced in a long time.

If he'd known coming to these smaller islands would prove so diverting he'd have come sooner. Athens was predictable and New York palled. Monte Carlo was passé and he wasn't in the mood for Rio's flamboyant parties.

What did appeal was his Nereid.

He liked that she didn't gush when he appeared. That she treated him as an equal.

Even her addiction to appalling clothes intrigued him. He laughed, thinking of the difference between designer string bikinis and tatty shorts. Today's shorts were infinitely better for they clung close. The jagged hem rose high on one side, to just below her buttock, catching and holding his gaze as she walked away. Amazingly he found the sight of that extra sliver of thigh more arousing than either of the women who'd paraded naked on his yacht.

As for her T-shirt... It clung lovingly to her magnificent breasts and made him more than ever determined to pursue their acquaintance.

Besides, he'd never had a biologist.

Class act, Doukas. Ticking them off by profession now?

Strato breathed deep, ignoring the tang of self-disgust on his tongue. Far from ticking off professions he was intrigued by her chosen field.

Anyway, he set limits around his relationships for an excellent reason. If that meant those relationships seemed increasingly shallow and unsatisfactory, that was the price he'd pay. The alternative was impossible.

Yet he wondered what would happen if he chose not to swim in the shallows but to venture into deeper water. If he pursued a woman who seemed complex and challenging and far removed from what he was used to.

He was sprawled, legs stretched out beyond the small table, his attention not on the sea but on the door to the hotel.

A little thrill wound its way down Cora's spine then around to her breasts and lower as their eyes locked.

He sat up as she approached. Did he notice she'd taken time to brush her hair? She'd wanted to change her clothes too but pride forbade it. His ego was big enough without her primping.

Cora recalled those times Doris had set her up to meet some prospective boyfriend. Inevitably when Cora appeared, Amazonian in height and stature, usually taller than the stranger Doris had invited, the guy would stare in dismay.

Then there were the ones drawn to Cora's generous figure. Whose eyes devoured her so eagerly her skin crawled.

Her skin didn't crawl now.

Poseidon's gaze might be meshed with hers but she hadn't missed that all-encompassing survey. He'd seen *and* approved. Instead of being discomfited, she revelled in his interest.

Why? That was the million-dollar question.

Cora moved between the tables, head up. Her shoulders were back, not curving forward as if trying to minimise her chest.

Bizarre that she should react like this to a stranger's gaze when blatant sexual interest usually annoyed her. This time she felt something like pride. Delight. Anticipation at spending time with him.

'Here you are.' She placed their tiny coffee cups, glasses of water and a plate of biscuits on the table and took a seat opposite him.

'You've been baking?'

Cora laughed, the sound a little too loud. 'Hardly.

I'm no domestic goddess. These are Doris's. Try one. The combination of honey and walnuts is delicious.'

He took one and bit into it, still holding her gaze. And, like yesterday when she'd watched him eat, Cora felt something flutter to life inside her. Something powerful and utterly feminine that she hadn't experienced in ages.

She'd told herself Poseidon couldn't be as attractive as she remembered and even if he were, it had to be surface gloss, the sort of shallow gloss she'd been inoculated against with Adrian and his friend.

Yet she looked at this man and felt something visceral. A yearning she couldn't identify.

She blinked and looked away, reaching for her coffee cup. Suddenly even sitting across the tiny table from him felt like an act of recklessness.

'So, you're not a cook. I assume you're a biologist?'

Cora looked up into that steady gaze and was momentarily lost. She had the weirdest floating sensation, as if she'd dived into warm, tropical waters and forgotten her bearings.

'Your T-shirt.' His words fractured the fantasy as he nodded towards her top. 'Or isn't it yours?'

She shook her head. 'It's mine and I am…was a biologist. A marine biologist.' She stifled momentary sadness. She didn't regret coming here. Her father needed her and that trumped everything. Theirs had always been a close-knit family.

Poseidon nodded. 'This must be a fascinating location to work. Isn't there a turtle nesting site around here somewhere?'

There was and its precise location was a carefully

kept secret. Even though she thought she saw real interest spark in his eyes.

'Yes, it is fascinating. Though I'm not working as a biologist at the moment.' She reached forward and took one of the biscuits, biting into it, appreciating the sweetness.

When she met his gaze again he was watching her mouth. Not leering, yet with an intensity that made her supremely self-aware.

'That's right, your father's been unwell. So you're helping here?'

'Yes. What about you? What do you do?' She knew all the locals, or thought she did. He had to be a visitor.

He shrugged in a lazy movement that drew her attention to the strength in his broad shoulders and powerful chest. 'Right now? As little as possible.'

So he was on vacation.

'What's your name?' His deep voice took on a different quality. Like whisky—warm with a rough edge that nevertheless slid easily through her. She had a premonition she could grow addicted to the sound of it.

'Cora. Cora Georgiou.'

'Cora.' His mouth lifted the tiniest fraction at one corner and in response she felt a blast of heat right through her middle. 'I like it. It's a good name for a Nereid.'

'A sea nymph?' She snorted and shook her head. 'Hardly. They're usually depicted on more delicate lines.'

He tilted his head to one side and Cora had the impression that he wasn't sizing up her body so much as exploring her mind.

It was an unsettling sensation. So few of the men

she'd known bothered with the cerebral. They took one look at her body and categorised her as either over-sized and therefore dismissible or an easy lay.

Yesterday she'd have put this man in the second category. Now she wondered if there was more to him than she'd thought.

'It's my fantasy, and as far as I'm concerned you're perfect for the role.'

Cora raised her eyebrows and sharpened her stare but he sounded genuine.

Her mouth curled wryly as she realised that, if he *had* been Poseidon, he'd have chosen sea nymphs to suit his personal preference.

'What is it?'

Cora shrugged. 'The coincidence that you thought of a Nereid and I thought of Poseidon.'

Too late she realised that would only feed his already healthy ego. Because Poseidon was always portrayed as the epitome of fit, powerful masculinity.

Yet instead of that puffing him up, she read genuine amusement in his glittering eyes. For a moment she felt a bond of shared humour, warm and…nice.

'I'm flattered. But I'm more interested in the fact our minds thought along similar lines.'

So was Cora. She couldn't recall the last time that had happened.

She sipped her coffee to hide her widening smile. The sharp taste of caffeine hit, revving her brain into gear and reminding her not to make assumptions.

'So what's *your* name?'

'Strato.' He paused. 'Strato Doukas.'

Cora felt her eyes widen.

Poseidon, indeed! For the god of the sea was also

known as Earth Shaker, responsible for earthquakes. And it felt right now as if the world tilted and shook around her.

Strato Doukas! Surely it wasn't possible.

Yet she'd heard via Doris that staff from his giant luxury cruiser had visited the harbour yesterday, buying fresh seafood and local produce. She'd even suspected this man was off that same yacht.

But Strato Doukas himself?

'*The* Strato Doukas?'

He shrugged. 'It's possible you've heard of me.'

Possible! The man was famed, or perhaps infamous, not just in Greece but far beyond. Mega-wealthy and renowned for his sybaritic lifestyle. He was rarely seen at the headquarters of his international logistics empire. Despite old stories of him taking his family's enterprise from moderately profitable to phenomenally successful, it was said he didn't bother with business any more.

These days he was too busy having a good time. The stories about him grew more and more salacious. Not that Cora read them, but Adrian and his friends had talked of the man, half envious and half admiring.

She took another sip of coffee, grimacing as the rich flavour turned bitter in her mouth.

'This doesn't seem your sort of place, Mr Doukas.'

Surely a multibillionaire playboy didn't frequent struggling little family hotels or pass the time with ordinary people like her.

Unless he was slumming it?

She remembered the gleam of amusement dancing in his eyes yesterday. She'd found it attractive. Too attractive. Now she realised he probably relished the novelty of her reaction to his nudity and his undeniably glorious body. Had he been laughing at her all the time? This man mixed with glamorous models and socialites. Women who'd look slim and elegant against her ample curves. No wonder he'd smirked over her ancient, baggy shorts.

The skin between her shoulders crawled and a shudder rippled down her spine.

She knew all about privileged men who found amusement with naïve women.

'Strato, please.' He paused, eyes narrowing when she didn't respond.

But suddenly the hints of shared intimacy, the repartee and amusement seemed one-sided rather than mutual.

Cora knew men like him didn't really view women like her as equals. Clearly he was bored. Then she remembered another snippet of gossip Doris had picked up in town. That Strato Doukas had not one but two Scandinavian lovers keeping him company on his luxury yacht.

She shoved her chair back so hard it screeched across the flagstones.

'I'm afraid I don't have time to sit and chat. There's a lot to do.'

He frowned.

To her horror, the expression didn't detract one iota from his attractiveness.

'It doesn't seem busy. You don't have many guests, do you?'

It was a reminder she didn't need. Business was poor with the economic downturn and the ferry from the mainland laid up for repairs. If things didn't improve it was only a matter of months before they'd have to close their doors permanently and sell. If they could find a buyer.

Then what would happen to her father?

Fear scraped her gullet.

And anger. Anger at this man who'd come here for light relief when his sophisticated playmates palled. As if Cora was some diversion.

What hurt most was realising how willingly she'd played along. How fascinated she'd been by this man. How eager.

'Nevertheless, I'm busy. You mightn't realise it but a lot of hard work goes on behind the scenes to provide the comforts others take for granted.'

His frown became a scowl and any trace of indolence disappeared from his big frame.

'You think I don't appreciate hard work?'

'I'm sure you appreciate a lot of things, Mr Doukas.' Like orgies with Scandinavian models and amusing himself with the yokels for a bit of variety. 'Now, if you'll excuse me I need to go. But please, take your time. The coffee is on the house.'

She'd taken a single step when he rose.

'Wait.' Instead of lazy indolence there was a note of command in that deep voice and, despite her intentions, Cora responded to it, halting.

When he spoke again the authoritative note was gone, or at least masked by a coaxing tone. 'I'd much rather you stayed.'

Cora shook her head. Her heart hammered high in her chest. 'I'm afraid that's impossible.'

He moved to stand before her.

She could walk around him yet his absolute stillness and that stare held her where she was. Once more she had the sensation he saw more than she wanted. Strange that a man renowned for his devotion to personal pleasure should have such a searching gaze.

'Why, Cora? Because you really have work, or because you're afraid of me?'

'Afraid?' Her chin jerked high and her hands planted on her hips. 'I'm not afraid of any man.'

No man had the power to hurt her any more. Because forewarned was forearmed. She'd never again be so gullible.

'No? Then maybe you're afraid of this, between us?' He raised his hand in a gesture that encompassed the pair of them.

For a second Cora felt relief that she hadn't imagined that connection between them. The invisible thread of shared amusement and camaraderie that had attracted her even more than his gorgeous body and bone-melting smile.

But it was no such thing. He was a handsome, too handsome, man with an aura of potent masculinity that would attract any woman. He'd set out to snare her and she'd fallen for it. Because he wanted a little rustic entertainment.

'There's nothing between us, Mr Doukas.'

He moved so fast she didn't have time to back away. Suddenly they were standing toe to toe and she had to arch her neck to maintain eye contact.

Cora couldn't remember ever being close to such a man. So much bigger than her, all powerful muscle and brooding intensity. The heat of his tall frame enveloped her.

Yet it wasn't fear she felt as he scowled down at her.

It was jubilation. And against her better judgement, anticipation.

A voice in her head told her she was mad. Reckless. Asking for trouble.

But she was no longer a victim. She'd rather infuriate Strato Doukas than run from him. She'd rather feel the way she did now, challenging him, than turn her back on this glorious feeling.

'Isn't there? Are you absolutely sure, Cora? Because it feels to me as if we share…something.'

He lifted his hand, hard fingers spreading over her jaw, his thumb a mere heartbeat from her mouth.

Heat drenched her. Heat and want. So intense she didn't know what to do with herself.

She struggled to keep her voice even. Admitting he was right would be a fatal error. 'Sorry, Mr Doukas. You must be imagining it.'

His nostrils flared on an indrawn breath and something flashed across his features. It didn't look like anger.

'Maybe you're right. After all, what could we have in common?'

Cora didn't move. She couldn't, because while her brain told her to leave, every cell in her body screamed that this was exactly where she wanted to be. A quiver ran through her as she waited, watching. Then she felt a band of warmth around her waist. He'd looped his arm around her. 'Unless, of course, it's this.'

His head swooped down to hers and her lips parted on a silent sigh of relief.

CHAPTER FOUR

STRATO PAUSED, HIS mouth a bare breath from hers, reading her emotions. Disdain morphing into expectation. Eagerness so bright it was like petrol thrown on the fire of his own desire.

Her eyelids flickered and that lush mouth opened a fraction. Not, he was sure, to spew contempt, but because, like him, she craved the kiss he delayed giving her.

He sensed part of her wanted to push him away. She was spiky and disapproving, and for the first time in for ever he found himself annoyed at being judged on his reputation. Usually Strato didn't give a damn what people thought of him. He lived life on his own terms because that was the only way to survive.

He could walk away, except those golden-brown eyes blazed up at him with such expectation.

His Nereid was complicated and he made it a policy never to bother with complicated.

And yet...

And yet he couldn't move back.

Couldn't release her. Because something dark and primal inside refused to let go.

The urge to taste her mouth became a need. What

had begun as teasing amusement became something elemental.

Why else would he put up with thinly veiled insults? As if this woman had the right to criticise him?

Was that why he held back? Forcing her to acknowledge that, far from trying to escape his hold, she was breathless with desire. Her breasts rose and fell with short, choppy breaths and her woman's scent, warm and rich, took on a deeper tang. Arousal. His nostrils twitched appreciatively.

Taking his time, Strato bent and set his open mouth on the pleasure point where her shoulder met her neck, nuzzling. Then, as the texture and taste of her filled his senses, sucking greedily at her satiny flesh.

She gasped, stiffening then instantly sinking against him, bending her neck to one side to allow him free access. She tasted like the distillation of summer—heat, sunshine and golden honey with a touch of sea salt.

Her hands fastened on his upper arms, fingers digging into biceps so needily that his arousal notched higher.

Elation filled him, and the expectation of profound delight to come. Despite her dismissive attitude, Cora had surrendered. She would give him exactly what he wanted.

Nuzzling his way up her neck, Strato registered her little hums of encouragement. Would she be vocal when they were naked together? This was a passionate woman. Not one worried about getting messy hair or trying to second-guess his every move. From her responsiveness he guessed she'd meet him halfway in any erotic venture.

His erection stirred in anticipation and was rewarded

with the press of her soft body. Cora moved her hips restlessly and he dropped his palm to her buttocks, pulling her hard against him.

There.

Better.

But he wanted far more.

Strato trailed kisses to corner of her mouth and she turned her head, lips seeking his.

So much for rejection. He stifled a huff of triumph, settling his mouth over hers.

And discovered something new.

Shock stormed his senses. His hold tightened and he braced his feet wider as an invisible blow rocked him from his scalp all the way down to the soles of his feet.

The taste of her, the melting sweetness of their mouths fusing, was a revelation.

He scrambled to gather his wits and catalogue the difference between this and past experience but his thoughts wouldn't fix on anything except a silent mantra of *Cora, Cora, Cora.*

And *more, more, more.*

Strato took her mouth and she reciprocated, welcoming, inviting and demanding.

She gave as much as he took and more, leaving him wanting so much more than a kiss. He wanted all of her, all to himself. He wanted to give her everything he had, not because he always felt duty-bound to please a lover, but because nothing less than everything would do.

Not with her.

He wrapped both arms around her, gathering her close so their bodies melded. She was a perfect fit. Strato could kiss her for hours and not get a crick in his neck and the feel of her voluptuous curves up close made him desperate to explore in minute detail.

The thought of their bodies joining…

He bowed her back over his arm and she clung, her mouth mating with his as if they'd been lovers for ever.

That was what felt so different. The ease and rightness of them together. As if they'd done this before and their bodies already knew each other intimately.

Strato's belly tightened and his groin grew heavy as he devoured her with languorous intent. He wanted Cora as he couldn't remember wanting any woman. But he had enough functioning brain cells left to realise that couldn't be here and now.

Regretfully he lifted his head, rejoicing in the way she rose against him, following his mouth, trying to prolong their kiss.

Oh, yes, my beauty. Soon. Very soon.

His breath came in great gusts and his muscles burned from the tension of standing still instead of hoisting her over his shoulder and carting her to the pier. They could be back on the yacht in fifteen minutes and naked in his bedroom fifteen seconds later.

Her eyes opened and it was like sinking into a pool of molten gold. Strato had never seen anything as powerfully enticing as that heavy-lidded stare and her lips, swollen and deep pink from passion.

Something twisted his gut. Something unfamiliar. Strato ignored it and concentrated on his next move.

'I want—'

Her finger on his lips stifled his words. Even that, a gesture not in itself erotic, sent a tremor of longing through him.

For a second longer they stood body to aching body.

Then, on a sigh that sounded more like a groan, Cora stepped back and Strato let her slide out of his arms.

Instantly he felt bereft. He wanted to haul her back where she belonged, against him.

But this wasn't the place. Not with her father likely to appear at any moment. Seducing his daughter in full public view wouldn't be a good move. Besides, Cora deserved better. Strato knew that ravishing this delectable woman thoroughly would require time and privacy.

She stood, staring up at him, slumbrous eyes, heaving breasts, hands hanging loose against the cut-off edges of her shorts. She wore no make-up and wasn't dressed to entice yet Strato couldn't conceive of any woman more attractive than she was right now.

Even with that prickly attitude, Cora was something special. In fact, he liked that she didn't make everything easy for him.

But the time for games was over. They both knew what they wanted.

'I'd like you to go now.'

Her words froze the smile forming at the corners of his mouth.

'Sorry?' He felt as if he were underwater, sound muted by the blood rushing in his ears.

She backed up a step and folded her arms. He wished she wouldn't. It tugged the cotton tight over those abundant breasts and made it hard to think about anything else.

'I'm not interested in what you're offering, Mr Doukas.'

Strato stiffened. Each carefully enunciated word hit like a slap. The only fire in her expression looked like anger.

Why was she angry? He'd given her a chance to walk

away before kissing her. She'd been a more than willing participant. It was too late to pretend otherwise. Her mews of pleasure had been impossible to miss, as had her enthusiastic body-to-body response.

He drew himself up and watched her eyes widen, fixing on his swelling chest. 'I don't recall making any offer, Ms Georgiou.'

At least not verbally.

She'd made one. The way she'd ground her pelvis against him spoke more clearly than any words.

Her eyes narrowed, her stare sharpening. 'My mistake.' She hefted a breath that looked painful, her mouth twisting. Strato wanted to reach out and...

What? Pacify her? Reassure her?

'Let's get one thing clear.' She paused. 'I'm not here to amuse you. If you're after a diversion don't expect me to provide it.' Her gaze skated down his body then back up, her expression dismissive. 'I hear you have quite a smorgasbord on your yacht, Mr Doukas. Don't come here looking for extras. I'm not interested in playboys.'

Strato felt every nerve and muscle stiffen. He relished a challenge but there were limits.

He crossed his arms, fighting the urge to reach for her and remind her how *interested* she was.

'That would be more convincing if you hadn't rubbed yourself against me like a cat on heat.' Deliberately he let his gaze drop to her proud breasts. 'Your nipples still give you away. I know for a fact you're not cold. The attraction is mutual.'

Her indrawn breath was a hiss. 'It didn't mean anything.' Her voice was hard and regret pierced Strato's annoyance. He wanted her soft and eager, not spitting ire. 'I admit I was…curious but I have more self-respect than that.'

His eyebrows arched and his mouth tightened. He didn't care what people thought of the way he lived his life but he wouldn't stand for direct insults.

What was her problem? All he'd done was kiss her. By her response she'd been hanging out for just that. Either they were phenomenally well-attuned physically or she was suffering from a desperate level of sexual frustration. Maybe both.

'Have you finished?'

She nodded, the movement jerky, her mouth a flat line.

'Good. Then let me clarify. If ever I make an offer to a woman, it's for shared pleasure, no strings attached. I have no interest in women who consider sex an insult or some sort of test. I find martyrs unattractive. If my lifestyle bothers you, look away. I don't have time for women who play hot and cold because they're too scared to confront what they feel.'

That hit home. He saw her register it like a blow. But instead of cringing back she jerked her chin up as if daring him to continue.

Strato was torn between admiration and annoyance.

She really was unique.

He moved into her personal space. She swallowed hard and he repressed a smile. Despite her veneer of outrage everything about her broadcast repressed hunger.

'I don't want someone who's afraid of herself or her physical needs. But if ever the other Cora returns, the sexy, confident woman who kisses like a goddess, let me know. *That* woman I'd like to know better.'

He let that sink in, watching with gratification as

Cora's pupils dilated. 'I'd gladly offer *that* woman the most memorable interlude of her life. I'll be on my yacht. The smorgasbord is gone so there'd be just her and me. And more rapture than she's ever known.'

Strato didn't wait for a response but strode away.

Two weeks later he stood on the terrace of his Moroccan hotel suite, watching the sun sink over the sea in apricot and amber splendour. When he turned he had a perfect view of the Atlas Mountains. The best money could buy.

The fountain beside him and the exclusivity of his accommodation in the gracious palace-turned-hotel meant he couldn't hear the noise of the opening night party.

Which suited him. Because, now he was here, he found he wasn't in the mood to party.

You've got it all and still you're not satisfied?

He stared at the glass in his hand.

What was wrong with him? The ennui that had dogged him was worsening.

For a week he'd stayed on his yacht, expecting Cora to contact him, his frustration increasing daily. Finally he'd headed to Canada on the spur of the moment for white water rafting, then Africa for off-road racing.

Neither had dimmed his discontent.

Strato had accepted this invitation anticipating the usual distractions. A sophisticated atmosphere. Like-minded acquaintances and enough gorgeous, willing women to entice any man.

Amber Harris, the sexy actress he'd met in the Bahamas, had greeted him in the lobby when he arrived. Her welcome had been warm and the invitation in her eyes and voice abundantly clear.

Then there was the French socialite he'd met on the ski slopes last year. Nadine had wit, charm and a lithe athleticism that appealed to his earthier side. She'd rung to check he was coming to this party, but he couldn't see himself beginning a liaison with her or Amber.

As for the sultry Brazilian singer taking the world by storm, maybe six months ago he'd have been diverted by her obvious interest.

Now though...

He swallowed his drink and put the empty glass down with more force than necessary.

Strato was unsettled. For years he'd had everything he wanted. Success. Wealth. Luxury. Beautiful companions. Yet increasingly he felt dissatisfied.

Globetrotting, extreme sports and self-indulgence palled, leaving what?

His dead uncle would have called him an empty shell of a man, refusing to create a family to which he could pass his wealth. His dead aunt would have looked at him with sad eyes and prayed he'd find peace and a good woman.

As if Strato would ever find that sort of peace.

His aunt and uncle, of all people, should have understood the baggage he carried made that impossible. How could they not have understood?

Thinking about a family of his own, of settling down with a woman, good or otherwise, curdled his belly and created a seam of sweat across his hairline and down his spine.

Bile rose in his gullet and Strato stalked to the edge of the terrace, needing to move. To escape the grave-yard of memories beginning to stir.

He shoved his hands in his trouser pockets and told

himself he'd feel better when he joined the others and lost himself in the usual distractions.

Except he knew, as he'd known for a fortnight, that it wouldn't work.

Whenever he thought of losing himself in a woman it was his Nereid who came to mind.

His pulse quickened as he remembered the flash of humour and even the glint of disdain on her features. Remembered the sway of her hips as she walked along the sand and the feel of her hourglass figure against him. Her taste, like nectar from the gods...

His listlessness wasn't boredom. It was because he wanted *her*. Cora. And no one else.

He wanted her to eat her disapproving words and beg for the pleasure only he could give her. Pride still smarted at her dismissal.

He wanted more of her banter, her quick intelligence, even her feisty attitude.

Almost as much as he craved her body.

With a sigh of resignation he hauled out his phone and dialled his head of security.

'Petro? I want everything you can get on Cora Georgiou.' He detailed everything he knew about her.

'This woman's bothering you?'

'No.' Strato almost laughed. She was, but not in the way Petro meant. 'She's not a security threat. But I want a full dossier. History, employment, financial situation. Anything and everything, and I want it straight away.'

'I'll get onto it.'

Strato ended the call and tossed the phone onto a seat. He rolled his shoulders, feeling the stiffness that had settled in his bones after two weeks of being denied what he wanted.

Jaded, spoiled and tainted too. Is it any wonder she doesn't want you, Doukas?

He had the unnerving suspicion that when Cora Georgiou looked at him she saw more than anyone else. Not the hedonist or the head of one of the world's most successful logistics companies, but right down to the nothingness deep inside. To the dark maw of dread and hollow emptiness that most of the time he managed to ignore.

At thirty-three he'd had twenty-five years to camouflage it. To appear like everyone else. Sometimes he went whole days without thinking about it, deliberately diverting himself with work and play and one enticing distraction after another.

But though he still worked, he'd achieved a level of success where he could delegate most day-to-day decisions and he always employed the best. As for distractions, they didn't gratify as they once had.

Maybe you only want her because you can't have her. Because if you have her you'll feel like you've conquered the emptiness for a little longer. So it won't consume you.

Strato's expression set in a scowl.

He prided himself on his honesty but sometimes self-reflection was overrated.

He toed off his loafers and hauled his shirt over his head. A few quick movements and his clothes dropped to the flagstones. He strode across the sun-warmed terrace and dived into the pool.

What he needed wasn't a party. He needed to numb his mind with exertion until Petro came through with his report and Strato could make his next move.

CHAPTER FIVE

'CORA, YOU NEED to come outside.'

Quickly she minimised the financial spreadsheet on the computer before it caught her father's eye. He was stressed enough without seeing her pore over their stubbornly bad projections for the summer.

She turned on the swivel chair and smiled. 'I thought you were heading to the harbour to meet your friends?'

Usually they came here, the older men spending hours on the shady terrace, setting the world to rights over coffee and backgammon. But today they were going to inspect the new motor on Niko's son's fishing boat.

'I am. I got delayed.'

From his grin, it wasn't some chore that had held him up. Cora saw his shining eyes and the way he stood with his shoulders back and felt her heart twist in her chest.

The last few months, recovering from two heart attacks and burdened by financial worry, her darling father seemed to have aged a decade. Now though, he looked almost as strong and healthy as he'd once been.

'What is it?' She rose and went to him. He gathered her hands in his gnarled ones and kissed her cheek. The reassuring scents of coffee and mints enveloped her. The same scents that coloured her earliest memories.

She squeezed his hands. It was so good to see him looking happy.

'Someone to see you, out on the terrace.'

'Who is it?' She wasn't expecting visitors.

Her dad winked and his smile grew. 'Someone you'll want to see. We've been having a good chat. But I need to get on now.' He tugged her hand. 'Come. Don't dawdle. We don't keep guests waiting.'

Whoever it was they'd impressed her father.

But to her surprise, when they reached the end of the corridor, her dad kissed her on the cheek and headed for the hotel's front entrance, motioning her towards the doors that led onto the terrace.

He wasn't even going to introduce her? Which meant it was a friend waiting. Eagerly she pushed open the door, wondering who'd come for a surprise visit.

She rounded a corner and slammed to a halt, heart pounding.

Surely not.

Cora told herself she was imagining things, that the bright sunlight dazzled her vision. Because she couldn't be seeing Strato Doukas sitting with his legs stretched out, sipping coffee and taking in the view of the bay.

Strato Doukas would never return here, not after what she'd said to him. Besides, the chef from his yacht who'd come into harbour yesterday for supplies had mentioned his boss had flown out and wasn't expected back soon.

Did she gasp or did he sense her presence?

Mirrored sunglasses turned in her direction and heat scorched her skin. Not just her cheeks and throat but across her breasts and stomach and deeper, right down in her feminine core.

'Cora.' Just that in a voice that sounded like a caress, its deep notes sliding through her and creating disturbing eddies of awareness.

She took a slow breath. None of this made sense. Especially the fact her father thought she *wanted* to see this man.

She turned her head but a swift scan showed the terrace was otherwise empty. In fact the whole hotel was empty, she realised, her dad on his way to the harbour and Doris spending the morning helping a friend who was recovering from illness. Their current guests, a couple of couples, had headed to the other side of the island.

Cora's pulse seemed to slow and the air in her lungs thicken.

'What are you doing here?'

One dark eyebrow rose but he looked more speculative than annoyed. 'Drinking coffee. Your father makes a particularly fine one.'

Protective instincts stirred. She wanted to tell him not to talk about her father. Or talk *to* him.

Slowly she paced across the flagstones. 'What did you say to my father?'

Strato pulled out a chair. 'Sit down and I'll tell you.'

He was maddeningly at ease and Cora was too aware of her emotions, anger, suspicion and…surely not eagerness?

Because she'd thought she'd never see him again.

And because, despite everything she knew about indulged, selfish rich men, she'd missed the sizzle in her blood when he was around. She'd even missed that intense awareness of her own femininity.

Whatever his game she wasn't interested. But she had to find out why he was here. What lies he'd told her father. She yanked the chair further out from the table and sat down, crossing her arms.

'There. That wasn't so hard, was it?'

'I have work to do, Mr Doukas. I can't spare long.'

'Really?' He took off his glasses and fixed her with a piercing stare that pushed her back in her seat. She'd told herself his eyes couldn't be nearly as mesmerising as she remembered, but they were. 'Surprising when you have so few guests and no prospect of many in the near future.'

Digesting his words took longer than it should have.

'How do you know about our bookings?'

He lifted his shoulders. 'I made it my business to find out.'

Cora opened her mouth then shut it again, too stunned to think of a riposte. He shouldn't even *be* here. Why bother to investigate their small family-run hotel? It didn't make sense. It wasn't the sort of place a billionaire took an interest in.

As she met that unblinking stare unease feathered her backbone. She didn't like the feeling that things careered out of her control.

Her hackles rose as she sensed a threat. 'What have you done?'

She leaned forward, unable to suppress foreboding, even when he spread his hands, palm up, and shrugged.

'Nothing.'

Cora didn't believe him. His expression might be innocently amiable but there was nothing innocent about this man.

'Then why are you here? Other than to drink coffee?'

'To see you, of course.'

Cora reminded herself she wasn't interested. Yet there was no denying her quiver of excitement. Part of her had regretted his departure. The part that had actually considered heading out to his status-symbol yacht and taking him up on his offer.

To have the most memorable interlude of her life. And more rapture than she'd ever known.

What woman wouldn't be tempted?

Especially as she was pretty sure Strato Doukas could deliver exactly that. If only a little of the gossip about him were true he was well versed in the art of lovemaking.

Such thoughts circled through her mind each night as she lay restless and frustrated in her lonely bed, even though her saner self knew she'd regret giving in to such an impulse.

He'd haunted her. The rumble of his deep voice. The light in his eyes when he'd shared a joke with her. The times when it had felt as if they were on the same wavelength, totally attuned.

The feel of his magnificent body hard and shockingly aroused against her. The bliss of his kiss.

She swallowed hard, remembering it all. And to be told she kissed like a goddess! Even though she knew it was a line he must have used with others, Cora's defences had trembled.

She smoothed damp palms across the cotton covering her thighs.

At least, for a change, she looked presentable in a bright summer dress.

Except she wasn't trying to attract him! She stiffened and sat straighter. 'What are you up to?'

'Are you always so suspicious?' His expression remained unreadable but his eyes danced.

'Are you always so devious?'

His mouth crooked up, revealing that beckoning groove in his cheek, and Cora's heart beat faster. Because his amusement felt approving, like shared merriment. Not a laugh at her expense.

'That's harsh, Cora. I might strategise but I'm honest.' He paused, his eyes on hers. 'Can you say the same? Or are you still trying to deny the sexual charge between us?'

Cora's chin jerked up. 'There are more important things than sexual attraction.' Belatedly she realised what she'd admitted and silently cursed her choice of words.

'Now we're making progress. What's important to you, Cora?'

'Family. Loyalty. Honesty.'

Probably all things he wasn't interested in.

He nodded. 'I can promise you loyalty and honesty, for the time we're together. As for family, I don't have any and I don't intend to settle down with a wife and children. *Ever.* It's important to remember that.' Something flashed in his eyes but before she could identify it he continued. 'However, I appreciate your desire to support your father.'

What did her father have to do with this?

'You speak as if we're going to be together.' Cora's voice rose.

Did he really think she'd change her mind? What was wrong with the man? It must be a case of wanting something because he'd been told he couldn't have it. It meshed with what she knew of his type.

Cora's lip curled. 'I thought I'd made it clear that won't happen. I don't even like you.'

It wasn't true. She liked him too much. But she knew men like him, spoiled, vain men who thought they could take whatever they wanted but didn't appreciate what they took so greedily. Cora valued herself too highly to be taken in by such a man again.

Strato shrugged, not looking in the least perturbed. 'I can live with that. I'd rather have your passion.'

Her mouth dried as wonder filled her. That she was having this conversation with Strato Doukas of all people!

She stiffened in her seat. 'It's not on offer. *I'm* not on offer, Mr Doukas.'

This time his smile held a secretive quality that stirred another premonition of danger.

'Ah, but you haven't heard my proposal, Cora.' He said her name in a deliberately slow, caressing tone that, despite her wariness, did disturbing things. She was sure something vital melted inside.

Her heart pattered faster. 'Go on, then. Tell me. Then you can go.'

But he seemed in no hurry, savouring the last of his coffee before setting down the tiny cup.

'Are you always this forthright?' he asked finally.

'Always.'

'Excellent.' He sat forward, making her even more aware of the shimmering magnetism of that big, powerful body. 'I like a woman who isn't afraid to ask for exactly what she wants. It can be very arousing in the right circumstances.'

In bed, he meant.

Cora swallowed as she read the carnal heat in his eyes and felt that same heat lick through her. But instead of rising to the bait she shook her head. 'You have one minute to tell me why you're here. Otherwise I'm leaving.'

'I thought that would be obvious. I want you, Cora. You know that. But since you refused to come to me I thought it time to provide a little…persuasion.'

The skin between her shoulder blades prickled. 'What sort of persuasion?'

Strato and her father had been talking. Her dad wouldn't have mentioned his precarious financial situation. Yet her hackles rose.

'What have you done to my father?' If he'd inveigled him in some way…

Strato lifted his hands palms out as if in surrender. 'No need to be so fierce. I've done nothing.'

Yet. The unspoken word hovered between them.

'Go on.' Her voice was thick with foreboding.

'I know you want me, Cora.' His words stole her voice. It was true, but the thought of him knowing it… 'Yet for some reason you deny yourself.' He paused. 'So I have a bargain for you. Something you want for something I want.'

Cora waited, her shoulders hitched high.

'Spend the next month with me on my yacht and I'll see to it that your father's hotel is filled to capacity till the end of the season. I plan to cruise the Ionian Sea then back to the Aegean and I can't think of a companion I'd rather have with me.'

She felt her mouth drop open in shock. She'd expected some sort of outlandish invitation but nothing like this.

'You're trying to bribe me into your bed.'

He shook his head emphatically. 'I'm creating an opportunity for us to get better acquainted. The rest is in your hands. You'd have your own stateroom and my word that I won't enter it except at your invitation. It will be your choice when we finally have sex.'

When, not *if*.

His arrogance outraged her.

A pity it also thrilled her.

Not because she liked arrogant men, far from it. But because the idea that sex between them was inevitable appealed on some primitive level she didn't even know she possessed.

He continued. 'The decision to have intimacy will be yours. I'm not interested in a woman who feels she has no choice.' His mouth curled in distaste. 'I'd never force a woman.'

His words rang with a steely quality that cut through her whirling thoughts. She *did* believe him. His body language as well as his tone proclaimed his sincerity.

Once more she was astounded by this flash of certainty about him. It had happened when they first met and it was happening again.

'You really believe no woman can resist your charm?'

'You find me charming?' He smiled and this time Cora knew he was laughing at her. 'That's a start.'

Cora shot to her feet and strode to the edge of the terrace, trying to calm herself, but the idyllic view failed to soothe her. Her mind was too full of his outrageous narcissism.

When she swung round he was where she'd left him but he sat straighter, not as relaxed as his earlier pose suggested.

'And if after four weeks I still won't share your bed?'

He shrugged. 'I'm flexible, it needn't be in bed—'

'You know what I mean!'

The man was impossible.

Or maybe that was her unruly imagination, picturing them stretched naked together out on the white sand beach where they'd met. Or right here in the dappled shade. She pictured sitting astride him, sharing another of those mind-blowing kisses, riding him till they both found ecstasy.

'I said it would be your choice and I mean it, Cora.'

Yet he expected to seduce her. It was there in his eyes. Unfortunately for his schemes that look reminded her of another man who'd viewed her as his for the taking.

'You're assuming I'd be persuaded. What happens if you're wrong. If I went aboard…?' Because who wouldn't be tempted by this man and the prospect of a month of luxury exploring the seas around Greece? 'And then you discovered sex really is off limits?'

Strato spread his hands wide. 'That's a risk I'm willing to take. I actually *do* want your company, not just your body.' Heat flared at his words but she concentrated on reading his serious expression. 'Look at it this way. In a contest of wills, if you decide not to sleep with me, you win and I learn a lesson in humility. Now *that* would appeal to you.' He grinned. 'And if I win, then believe me, Cora, we'd *both* be winners.'

Scary how tempting it sounded. Outrageous but tempting. A reckless part of her revelled in the idea of besting him in such a battle of wills. She'd like to puncture that ego, just a little.

'It's ridiculous. Even someone as rich as you wouldn't waste your money helping a small-time hotel owner out of debt.'

Strato's head cocked to one side in that assessing way she'd come to know. For a long time he said nothing, leaving her too aware of the hurried in-and-out rush of her breathing, her hands fisted at her sides, and the curling heat low in her pelvis that she assured herself he couldn't know about.

'Why not? As you say, I've got plenty of money to spend as I wish.' Another lift of his shoulders and outspread hands.

'You actually mean it?'

'Say the word, *Coritsa*, and the bookings will start.'

The diminutive pet version of her name sounded like a caress in his dark velvet and whisky voice. Nothing at all like when her father or Doris called her that. It took her a moment to gather her wits.

'Even you can't conjure guests out of thin air.'

His complacent smile should have annoyed her but this time Cora found it almost reassuring. 'I head a very large company. I've decided to offer vacations as performance bonuses, and for employees recuperating from serious illness.'

'That's very generous.' In other words, she found it hard to believe.

'I expect loyalty and dedication from my staff but in return I offer excellent conditions. It's how we attract and retain the best.' He paused. 'As for the bonus holidays, the suggestion came from a recent staff survey and my advisers believe in it.'

No humour in his voice now. Cora heard pride and the voice of a man who knew what he was talking about. Strato Doukas didn't sound like a lazy playboy now, but a corporate manager. Like a man who'd taken his family transport company and turned it into a multinational corporation.

Cora hadn't been able to resist looking him up online. She'd tried to ignore the breathless gossip about his debauched lifestyle, curious instead about the man himself. Surprisingly for someone at the centre of so much publicity, there wasn't much of substance. He'd grown up in Athens but there was little information on his early life. By his late teens he'd been learning the family business, eventually inheriting it and expanding it enormously. These days, though, others ran the company while Strato Doukas swanned from one pleasure spot to another, living off the profits.

Except what he'd said indicated he still took an active interest in the business. Even more curious.

'You'd really do all that to get me on your boat?' She didn't know whether to feel complimented or insulted.

'I don't waste time doing anything against my will, Cora. Life is too short.'

Once more she had a fleeting glimpse of something more than uber-confidence in his expression. For a second Cora saw something stark in his gaze. Then he smiled and she was too dazzled to think straight.

'An offer too good to refuse, eh?'

Cora jammed her hands onto her hips. 'What lie did you tell my father? He seemed…happy after meeting you.' Which he wouldn't be if he understood Strato's intentions.

'I told him how much I wanted you to accompany

me. I explained I planned an extended cruise and that I'd value your marine biology expertise, particularly when we visit marine reserves.'

Cora forced down a fillip of pleasure at the thought of returning to the work she loved. 'So you lied.'

Strato shook his head. 'I told him the truth. I'll look forward to seeing the places we visit through your eyes. I suspect you'd give me a new perspective. As for our sexual magnetism, that's a private matter between us.'

'He thinks you're *hiring* me for my expertise?'

'I could pay you a cash salary, but I thought you'd prefer to see the hotel full.'

He was right. Cora shook her head, trying and failing to take it all in.

'It's a crazy idea. No one would go to so much effort to get...' Her words died under the weight of that steady stare.

She told herself it had to be a joke. But he looked serious. Goosebumps rippled over her arms and she rubbed her tight flesh. He wanted to buy her.

It was outlandish. Unbelievable.

Intoxicatingly exciting.

She blinked and looked away, past the tamarisks to the harbour town on the other side of the bay, so quiet now with the economic downturn and the lack of regular ferry services.

If they could hang on till next year bookings would pick up and they'd manage to repay the debt. But next year was a long time away. By then her dad would be bankrupt and heartbroken, losing the hotel he and Cora's mother had run together.

'How do I know you'll follow through with your promise? That the guests will come?' She turned around.

Strato sat forward, elbows on the table, as if sensing victory. The sight made Cora feel trapped and angry. And more determined to withstand this man's terrible magnetism.

'Check your reservation requests in an hour and you'll see that I mean it. While we're away you can call your father every day. If I renege on my promise, I'll have you brought straight back here.'

Could she trust him?

The sparse information available about his work style indicated a man who followed through on promises. Whose word was his bond. But that had been in corporate deals. This was something else.

She caught the direction of her thoughts and her breathing fractured. Was she really thinking about agreeing?

As if sensing her confusion, Strato rose from his seat. 'You need time to consider. I'll be back this afternoon for your answer.'

He moved to stand before her. Close enough that she could read the speculation in his eyes and almost feel the warmth of his tall frame.

'Have a bag packed, *Coritsa*. We leave today.'

Before she could conjure a suitable response, Strato turned and walked away, that lazy, loose-limbed stride deceptively fast.

Not once did he look back. Every movement reinforced his supreme assurance. That almost unbelievable confidence that he'd get his own way. She wanted to despise him for that yet instead was transfixed by the sight.

And by the yearning to throw aside life's hard-learned lessons and say *yes*. Yes, to sheer self-indulgent pleasure.

Because this man wasn't like Adrian. He might be a selfish, spoiled rich man. But, in offering her choice and negotiating, offering something of immense value for her time, he made her like an equal, not a plaything.

He turned an indecent, outrageous proposal into something almost acceptable.

She shook her head. Acceptable? She must be insane!

Cora's breath sawed in her lungs and she pressed her palm to her abdomen, trying to quell the hot, coiling tension of sexual desire.

In moments he was out on the pier, casting off. The motor started and the tender headed out across the bay.

Still Cora stood, feet planted where he'd left her.

It was only as the tender reached the yacht that she went inside, her thoughts awhirl.

Forty minutes later she opened the online reservations portal and found a request for accommodation from a familiar-sounding company. *His* company. The booking was for two double rooms, two singles and two of the new family rooms her father had added and fitted out at such cost. All the bookings were for three weeks, beginning next Monday.

With a couple of quick keystrokes she accepted the booking, her heart hammering. Half an hour later a sizeable deposit appeared in their account.

Cora sat back in her seat, wide eyes fixed on the positive balance.

He was serious.

Strato Doukas had the power to save her family home, her father's business and his pride. If she agreed to spend the next month with him.

What's the worst that can happen? You want him as much as he wants you. He's not pretending love or raising hopes of anything long term. He's been upfront with you from the beginning.

Not like Adrian.

Still Cora stared, refusing to make a decision.

Because this man made her feel too much. That was dangerous. She could get hurt if she gave in to his charm and phenomenal sex appeal. She'd be better off keeping her distance. Not seeing him again.

But the thought of him sailing away and never returning made her stomach cramp. And the idea of the hotel being sold by the bank to cover her father's debts made her hunch over welling nausea.

Finally, what seemed a lifetime later, Cora sat straight, her mind made up.

If the hotel was going to be full, and she wasn't going to be around to run it, they'd need to rehire trusted staff from the village. She reached for the phone.

CHAPTER SIX

STRATO CUT THE engine as the tender neared the yacht. Before either he or the waiting crew member could do it, Cora rose, balancing easily in the small boat, and secured it to the larger vessel.

Her movements were economical, betraying the ease of long practice. According to the report he'd received, she worked off boats all the time, and had even spent a season between research jobs crewing a luxury yacht.

But it wasn't her nautical skills that held his attention. It was the way her khaki capri pants clung to her hips and buttocks as she moved, the supple twist of her body and the swell of her full breasts against her top.

She left him breathless.

It was so long since any woman had stolen the air from his lungs that he couldn't remember it happening.

Careful, Doukas. These are uncharted waters.

As if he cared. He'd been in a lather of anticipation for days, since he'd decided to make her confront the magnetism between them.

He'd crossed to the shore in a state of mixed eagerness and anxiety.

Anxiety! Him! Because it was just possible this woman might reject his offer.

It was unheard of.

But his response to Cora Georgiou was unlike anything he'd known.

He'd tried to tell himself it didn't matter if he didn't bed her. If he couldn't capture that energy, that spirit and that sexy body in his arms. Or trade banter with her again in a way that made him feel energised, not enervated. Yet as he'd strode up to the hotel his heart had been in his mouth and his belly clenched as if anticipating a blow.

Till he'd seen her kiss her father in the doorway and stoop to pick up a single suitcase. Then Strato had felt a rush of relief.

The thought of not seeing her again, not discovering why she challenged and delighted him so, had disturbed him.

Cora reached for her case but he forestalled her, grabbing it before she could. Her fingers brushed his and a jolt of energy shot through him. And through her too. Her eyes widened and she curled her hand protectively close to her body as if that spark between them burned.

'Allow me.' Strato smiled as he gestured for her to go first. She felt this connection as much as he.

Cora's seduction would be swift and satisfying.

As well as carnal satisfaction, it would be a relief to conquer the unsettled mood he'd been in since they met. His reaction to her was surely heightened by uncertainty. Surely it would lessen with familiarity...

His thoughts frayed as she climbed up onto the yacht, all toned muscle and delicious femininity.

Did she really think covering herself from neck to calves would stop him appreciating her stunning body?

She couldn't be so innocent.

Yet Strato carefully suppressed his smile as he followed her. She was skittish enough without him making it obvious he wanted to take her straight to bed.

Skittish but delightfully aware of him.

Strato passed the surprisingly light case to his crew member with a word of thanks and turned to Cora. She might be at home aboard vessels but there was a quaint awkwardness about the way she stood, hands clasped, that pierced his smugness.

It reminded him that despite the sexual charge thickening the air, Cora had doubts about being here.

He stepped close and her head swung up, eyes wide.

Strato stopped and surprised himself. 'Why don't you have a rest before dinner? Vassili can take you to your stateroom.'

He'd intended to offer her champagne on deck as they watched the island slide by. But her wary expression and stiff pose made him feel strangely protective.

Of the woman he intended to seduce.

Another first.

'Thank you. I'd like that. It's been a busy day.'

Strato pasted on a smile, as if he didn't mind she'd agreed so readily. 'Vassili can give you a tour of the yacht so you can find your way around. I'll see you on the upper deck in an hour and a half.'

He stood, watching her go, revising his plan, telling himself it made sense to give her space. Instead of pushing her, which would make her dig her heels in, he'd keep his distance. Let her stew. Let her feel the torment of unfulfilled desire till she was desperate for him. Then she'd come to him.

Then and only then would he give her what her body craved.

* * *

Cora stared in the full-length mirror of her marble and glass bathroom and grimaced.

Seeing herself in such surroundings sent tremors of unease down her spine. She looked so ordinary, wearing a plain white top and khaki pants, her face devoid of make-up. So not at home in this extravagant setting.

She knew the women who stayed on yachts like this. Women who didn't work for a living, unless you called snaring and keeping a rich husband or boyfriend work. Women who'd shriek at wearing chain-store clothes or chipping their nails by doing actual physical labour.

It reinforced her suspicion that Strato was interested because she was a curiosity. She didn't fit the mould.

Her resolve strengthened. She wasn't about to become one of his women. If he thought she'd be so awed by luxury that she'd fall into his bed, he was about to learn a lesson.

Cora didn't fit here, unless it was as a deckhand, working to keep this superyacht in sparkling condition. It made Adrian's yacht, or more precisely his father's, look like a minnow beside a shark.

Her hand strayed to the smooth, sweeping lines of the custom-built vanity unit. She'd bet all the money she didn't have that the stone was Pentelic marble. Sunlight pouring through the large window highlighted a warm golden tinge to the stone she'd initially thought pure white.

Only the best for a man like Strato Doukas. Why wouldn't a billionaire demand the same stone as that used to create the Parthenon?

She shook her head, remembering her tour of this floating mansion. There'd been a pool and spa, several lounge rooms, small dining room, large dining room and a bar big enough to host all her village. A cinema, library, billiards room, sauna and an enormous gym and massage suite that, despite its pristine condition, had the air of being well used. She'd lost count of the state-rooms and that was without descending below decks to the staff quarters.

Cora brushed her hair then yanked it back in a tight ponytail. Then she wrapped it deftly around her fingers and secured it in a no-nonsense bun.

She wouldn't dress up for dinner. Soon Strato would tire of playing a game he couldn't win.

Because Cora wasn't the naïve woman she'd been before. Adrian had seen to that. Opulent yachts didn't impress her. For she knew about the men who owned them, their strain of seedy indulgence and sense of en-titlement.

Yet her nerves strung tight as she moved into her enormous stateroom and shuffled into her deck shoes. She felt too wired.

Rest had been impossible. She'd tried. Except lying on the king-sized bed she'd kept imagining Strato sprawled beside her, naked, with that devilish glint in his eyes and the smile that made her feel as if the two of them shared a secret.

Finally she'd got up and had a shower, hoping to cool her overheated body. But she kept visualising him there with her. Those long-fingered hands playing across her, that muscular body sliding against her as he—

With a huff of annoyance Cora opened her door and headed out to meet her host. Some bracing sea air would clear her head.

She found him on his private deck, along with a

table set for two, complete with a centrepiece of fragrant roses.

Cora wanted to curl her lip at the predictability of the romantic setting. Except it *was* beautiful. Not fussy but the best quality. The tablecloth wasn't snowy linen but a rustic cloth with a Greek key design that looked handwoven. The silverware shone and the glassware, while elegantly made, didn't teeter on overlong stems that would be dangerous on an unstable sea.

She noticed all that because she didn't want to notice *him*, over against the railing, looking out to sea as they cruised past a small island.

The view was spectacular, the sun low over the water, turning the air golden.

Finally, unable to resist, she slanted a look at Strato, her gaze snagging on his straight shoulders before roving further.

He hadn't changed for dinner either. In long shorts that hugged his buttocks and thighs, and a short-sleeved shirt that left his sinewy arms bare, he looked fit, strong and mouth-wateringly masculine. Even the way the breeze ruffled his dark hair enhanced his attractiveness.

He was talking on the phone and she caught drifts of conversation. To her surprise it seemed to be about labour negotiations in the Far East.

Not what she expected from a hedonist who spent his life chasing pleasure.

He turned, gaze colliding with Cora's, and something shifted inside her, as if he'd untied something vital.

'I have to go. We'll talk later.' Putting the phone away, he smiled, and that curling dimple appeared beside his mouth. 'Welcome, Cora. You feel rested?'

'A little.' It was a lie, but better than admitting her inner turmoil.

'Would you like a drink?' He lifted his glass of sparkling liquid and her nerves settled a little. Because now he was following a predictable pattern, trying to use champagne to turn this into a celebration and weaken her resolve.

'I'd rather have water, thanks.'

His eyebrows arched and his smile grew as he crossed to a bar. 'Good. That's what I'm having. Still or sparkling?'

Cora blinked. He was drinking water? And talking business? Was this the man who kept a harem on his yacht and spent the day lolling naked on the beach?

'Sparkling,' she croaked. It was easier when he acted to type. Then she could dismiss him, or try to.

When he turned and held out a glass, Cora's chest squeezed. Not in fear or dislike. But because, looking into those dancing eyes, she acknowledged what she'd tried to ignore.

She wanted to be here.

Wanted to bask in his smile and stand close to that imposing body that drew her like a swimmer to a warm current.

'Here's to a memorable cruise.' He clinked his glass against hers and Cora nodded and sipped.

That was the beginning of an utterly unexpected evening. At every turn Strato defied expectations.

They moved to the railing and he asked her about the island they were passing, what she knew of its history and the marine life in the area. From there the conversation headed to marine conservation areas in the region, the best places for diving, and her recommendations.

Strato mentioned some places he'd thought of visiting and asked her opinion.

Instead of flirting he conversed sensibly and listened to her responses. Gone was the teasing light in his eyes and his gaze didn't once drop below her neck. Cora found herself relaxing, slowly dropping her guard as they talked.

By the time they were at the table, feasting on fresh seafood and a bottle of crisp white wine from a small Greek vineyard she'd never heard of, she was no longer watching every word. For there was no sexual innuendo. No sly smiles. Just pleasant company in gorgeous surroundings. Even if she was constantly aware of the man opposite, her eyes drawn to his compelling features.

She sighed. 'The sunset is gorgeous from here. There's something about being on the water that makes it special.'

'I agree. It's the best place for sunrises and sunsets.'

Hours ago Cora would have scoffed at the idea of Strato being up to see the sun rise, but now nothing would surprise her.

She leaned back in her seat, enjoying the view, even if she had to work not to keep glancing back at the man opposite her. The sea looked like liquid silk, peach and an intense fluorescent pink that should have looked unreal against the gathering indigo.

Cora realised that for the first time in ages, she felt completely relaxed. Not stressing about the hotel or finances or how looming bankruptcy might affect her father's health.

If Strato hadn't sauntered into her life with his outrageous proposition, can-do attitude and phenomenal wealth, able to fill their hotel with a few phone calls, she'd be steeling herself to talk to her father about selling the family business.

She hated Strato's sense of entitlement, believing she'd fall into his hands, but the hard truth was he'd saved her father's business and, Cora believed, his life. For she feared her dad would fade away without the hotel that generations of his family had built.

Cora blinked, frowning as she realised how much she owed Strato. He'd given them the breathing space they needed to make good by the time next year's hopefully normal tourist season came around.

'What's wrong, Cora?' That deep voice caressed her, comforting yet exciting at the same time.

She took a moment to gather herself, conquering the weakness that made her want to lean into him, seeking comfort. Tonight it was too easy to forget he wasn't a friend.

'Thank you, Strato.' She met his gaze squarely. 'I didn't thank you for what you've done for my father, making it possible to keep the hotel running. That means a lot. I've been so worried about him.'

His eyebrows angled down as he frowned. 'I'm glad it's helped. I like him. But my motives are selfish. You know why I did it.'

His expression dared her to think well of him.

Cora nodded. 'I'm not likely to forget.' How often was a woman, particularly an ordinary working woman, propositioned in such spectacular fashion? She was no *femme fatale*.

Yet she didn't see that familiar speculative gleam in his eyes. The glint of sexual interest and invitation she'd associated with him from the first. He looked genuinely concerned she'd mistake him for someone benevolent.

Her mouth twitched.

'What's so funny?' He looked wary and that made her smile broaden.

'You. Worried I might mistake you for a good guy.'

He wasn't. He really, really wasn't.

His actions were prompted wholly by self-interest.

Yet he was upfront about it. He wasn't deceitful. Cora could cope with Strato's sort of selfishness. As long as she didn't fall into the trap of believing there was more to his actions than an attempt to get his own way.

'That's not the way I'm usually described.' His mouth rucked up at the corner in that almost-smile that had fascinated her from the first. She felt her breath slow and made herself look away.

'I can imagine.' She'd read the headlines.

'Would you be sorry to lose the hotel? If it weren't for your father?'

Cora shrugged. 'I can't imagine it not being part of my life. My earliest memories are there.' It had seemed a golden place when her mother was alive. Then, when it was just her and her father, they'd been a tight-knit unit, drawing on each other for strength as they fought grief and found a way to go on. 'It's been in the family for generations and it's a special place. We have guests who come back year after year.' Though fewer this year, due to circumstances beyond their control.

'Do you *want* to run a hotel?'

She shook her head. 'I'm used to it but, no, it's not my dream. Unless I could install a manager and spend most of my time working on a marine project.' She shifted in her seat. 'Sadly funding for marine research isn't easy to come by.' Which was why she'd done a stint working on a yacht. 'Especially not near our island.'

'So it's your father keeping you there.'

Cora slanted a look at Strato, surprised at his curiosity. Was he, like Adrian, feigning interest to make it easier to get her into bed? Yet that wasn't the vibe she got from the big man sitting there so relaxed, twisting his glass on the table.

'He isn't forcing me to stay. I want to. He's my father and I love him.'

The light changed. At least she assumed it was that, because for a second Strato's face darkened, turned stark and brooding. But a moment later the impression was gone and he looked just the same.

'How about you, Strato?' She felt hyper-conscious of his name on her tongue. 'Are you sentimental about your family home?'

'No.' The answer came swiftly. 'I don't have a family home.'

'Really? There's nowhere special you feel attached—'

'Nowhere. No family home, no family. And I'm not sentimental.'

Cora heard the warning note and stiffened. Gone was the companionable man she'd begun to relax with. Gone the easy conversationalist. His tone was as welcoming as a *Trespassers will be shot* sign and his features set hard.

Strato saw her double take, that instant of shock when she read the grimness he couldn't hide, and silently cursed.

He was used to deflecting interest in his personal life, and particularly the past, with ease. A casually dismissive comment, a change of subject and it was done. Tonight for the first time he could remember, that skill eluded him.

Because Cora touched a part of him that no one else did? Because he'd felt a flicker of jealousy over her relationship with her father and her obviously happy family life?

Strato dismissed the notion. His past was dead and buried. He didn't yearn for family. Instead the thought sent a glacial chill through him.

But he saw Cora's recoil and regretted his curt tone. A moment before she'd been relaxed and happy to share.

Pushing aside instinctive distaste, for he *never* spoke of this, he said, 'I was orphaned.' The words stuck like shards of glass in his throat.

Cora's tight features softened. 'I'm sorry. That must have been dreadfully hard.'

He made himself shrug, as if his neck and shoulders hadn't seized up. 'I was lucky enough to be adopted.' He paused and repeated, 'I was very lucky.'

It was what he'd told himself over and over. What others had said in those early days. Somehow, though, he'd never believed it.

'So you were happy with your adoptive parents?'

Another question he never answered in public. Not because his aunt and uncle had been anything other than kind, decent people, but because talk of family screwed him up.

'They cared.' He swallowed a mouthful of wine. 'They gave me stability and safety.' But no matter how hard his aunt in particular tried, they couldn't replace what he'd lost. 'My adoptive father took me into his business straight from school and taught me everything he knew. When he died I inherited the company and built it into what I have now.'

Cora watched a smile that wasn't really a smile stretch his features and felt the hairs rise on her nape.

Something was wrong. Something that turned this sexy, self-assured man into a shadow of himself.

It lasted bare seconds. He caught her gaze on him and sat straighter, his expression shifting into something approximating amusement.

At her or himself?

'Sorry. I don't talk about the past much. I prefer to focus on the present. And prospects for the future.' His intimate smile told her he was thinking of his goal of persuading her into sex.

Yet the blankness in his eyes belied that inviting smile.

She nodded, knowing it was time to change the subject. 'I understand that. So, are you going to tell me how you turned your adoptive father's medium-sized transport company into a global corporation?'

If she'd expected eagerness, she didn't get it. It seemed Strato wasn't the sort of man who needed to broadcast his success. Why would he? His wealth spoke for itself. Nevertheless, his body language changed as he refilled her glass and started talking, briefly outlining his strategies and successes and sharing some amusing anecdotes.

Even as she smiled and responded, fascinated by the different world he described, Cora's thoughts returned to the brief but real emotion she'd seen. The grim darkness that had engulfed him.

It had made her want to reach out to him. Not because Strato was the most attractive, charismatic man she'd ever met, but because for an instant she'd seen something that made her want to comfort him.

She couldn't shift the idea she'd had a glimpse of the man behind the headlines. A man who kept himself hidden.

Who was Strato Doukas? She could no longer put him in a box and label him as simply a shallow party animal. That was one side of his character. Maybe one he played up?

Or was she projecting because she wanted him to be more? Because the man she'd seen this evening was one she liked too much. One who intrigued her.

Strato confused her. She wanted to understand him—the man who thought he could bribe her into bed!

The trouble was, the longer they were together, the more she realised the idea wasn't as outrageous as she'd told herself. It was actually…tempting.

CHAPTER SEVEN

CORA LOWERED THE anchor of the small tender and turned on her bench seat to find Strato pulling out the snorkels. He hauled off his T-shirt, leaving her with a view of his tanned chest and sculpted torso. Of the slight fuzz of dark hair that accentuated the shape of his powerful pectorals. Of the way his lean, muscled form tapered to a flat belly and narrow hips.

She was so *aware* of him. Felt it like an electric charge humming from her fingertips to her toes.

That hadn't changed, despite discovering last night that he was more complex and intriguing than she'd first imagined.

Despite the fact that, all morning, as they cruised past a scatter of islands, Strato had kept his distance, allowing her space. When they were together he'd chatted without any hint of sexual interest.

It was a relief not to be pestered.

Yes, a relief!

She was *not* disappointed to be virtually ignored after she'd spent the whole night thinking of him.

Of him and her together.

Besides, Strato didn't ignore her. He'd been a perfect host. Offering every amenity, yet not fussing around her.

Not by so much as a sidelong glance or teasing comment had he made her feel uncomfortable.

She'd done that all by herself.

After a restless night in her vast bed, imagining how it would be to share it with him, Cora was strung too tight.

'You've changed your mind about swimming?' His voice cut through her thoughts and Cora yanked her gaze up from where it had stuck on his dark swim shorts and powerful thighs.

Heat warmed her cheeks. She'd been caught staring.

Yet when her eyes met Strato's his expression didn't register anything but mild curiosity.

No doubt lots of women checked out his body.

All the time.

Cora gritted her molars and told herself she'd have to do better if she were to maintain a pretence of not wanting him.

'No. I haven't changed my mind.'

She undid her shorts and rose a fraction off the seat to pull them down. Then she shucked off her deck shoes, placing them with her neatly folded shorts.

The sooner they were in the water, and she had something to concentrate on other than this man who could have modelled for a Greek god, the better.

Gripping the bottom of her T-shirt, she yanked it up and over her head and folded it, leaning down to place it with the rest of her clothes.

'You play dirty, Cora.' Strato's voice was low and a little rough, making her think of gravel and suede. At the sound of it her body softened as if caressed.

'Sorry?' She looked up to find him watching her.

This time, his gaze raked from the top of her scalp

down to her soles and back up again, lingering along the way before rising to focus on her face.

'I promised our affair would go at your pace, but then you wear a swimsuit with a front-opening zip. A *long* front-opening zip.' Strato shook his head, his expression mournful but his eyes hot. 'Underhand tactics, Cora, very underhand.'

She told herself she did *not* feel adrenaline pump through her blood at that look. As for the thrill tickling its way along her spine and down between her legs, making her shift on the seat...

'I'm sure you're used to seeing women wearing much less than this. It's a perfectly respectable one-piece.'

Because when she'd flung in clothes for this trip she'd avoided packing a bikini. She'd grabbed two one-piece swimsuits instead, telling herself she'd give Strato no encouragement.

He leaned back on his hands in a move that spread his shoulders and bare chest and made Cora swallow convulsively. He really was superbly made.

Just as well he didn't know she'd spent the night fantasising about him.

'True. But didn't you know there's a delightful piquancy about what's hidden from view? Topless string bikinis leave nothing to the imagination and I've lost my taste for the obvious.'

His voice dropped to a bass rumble that made Cora shiver. Not with fear but something like anticipation.

That tickle between her thighs strengthened, teasing, and it took real effort not to twitch where she sat. Because after a morning of treating her like a sister or elderly aunt, Strato was suddenly looking at her with blatant sexual appreciation. His nostrils flared as if scenting her arousal. The skin across his cheekbones tightened and those remarkable eyes looked slumbrous and secretive. Inviting.

Cora shook her head, making her tone as disapproving as she could. 'It's got a high neckline. It needs the zip for access.'

A slow smile began at the corner of his mouth then travelled across his face. 'Precisely. It's designed to tempt a man into reaching out and tugging that silver loop down...' His gaze dropped from the base of her throat to her breasts and slowly, infinitely slowly, to the spot low on her abdomen where the zip ended.

Cora searched for a dismissive response but her throat had dried. She felt her nipples bead and thrust towards him and hoped the black fabric would hide the sight.

'It makes me think...' his eyes locked on hers and lightning sheeted through her out of the clear sky '...you wore this to tempt me.'

She swallowed. There was an element of truth in that. She'd pulled out both swimsuits this morning, taken one look at the brown with its traditional style and dull colour and couldn't bring herself to put it on. Because the black with the high-cut legs, the sharp angle in towards her neck that left her shoulders completely bare, and its long zip, made her feel feminine and powerful. Sexy.

She'd told herself she didn't want to attract his attention but at the first chance she'd dressed to catch his eye.

What did that say about her determination to keep her distance?

She *liked* it when Strato looked at her with that smouldering stare.

She *liked* feeling desirable.

Cora had warned herself not to weaken when he tried to seduce her. She hated the idea of being manipulated. Yet this wasn't him seducing or manipulating but her demanding his attention.

Pride and common sense told her not to fall for his practised charms because all he offered was shallow physical passion. But the rest of her clamoured that physical passion with Strato would do her fine, thank you very much!

She'd been sensible so long, guarding her heart. At least with him there was no pretence of hearts being involved. It was about lust and for the first time in her life Cora discovered how phenomenally powerful that could be.

Powerful and attractive.

Her whole body seemed to throb in time with her quickening pulse. Stoically she ignored it.

'I dress to please myself, Strato.' That was true. Seeing the rampant appreciation in his eyes made her feel wonderful. Even if it was wonderful tinged with danger. 'But if you'd rather not swim with me—'

His raised palm stopped her. 'On the contrary. I'm looking forward to it very much.'

He passed her a mask and snorkel and she took them, carefully not touching his fingers.

Did he notice? She feared Strato noticed most things. Cora was only too ready to get into the water and away from this conversation. She primmed her mouth and went through the usual safety checklist with him.

For, despite his seduction scheme, ostensibly she was here because of her marine expertise, helping him explore an area he didn't know. It salved her pride to think she was different from the other women he took on his yacht. More than simply someone to flirt with.

'Remember, stay close,' she concluded. 'Don't go into one of the sea caves alone.'

The sea was calm today but accidents happened and she was the expert. If she didn't know where he was…

'Don't worry, *Coritsa*. I intend to stick to you like glue.' His face was grave but the gleam in his eyes made her breath catch and her knees wobble.

Cora grinned as she hauled herself up onto the sun-warmed rock above the tiny, secluded inlet. What a brilliant afternoon. She rolled her shoulders, filled with that good feeling of muscles well used, and bent to scoop up a towel.

'That was fantastic!' Strato's voice made her turn in time to see him hoist himself up out of the water and onto the broad rock platform in a demonstration of upper-body strength that she envied.

The sight of him, all streamlined strength and toned masculinity, was enough to dry a woman's throat. Even one who hadn't been immersed in salt water for hours.

His eyes snared hers, black eyelashes spiked around bright green eyes, and the blaze of exhilaration she saw there stole her breath. Water dripped from his hair, running down his features and his broad chest and for an insane moment she wanted to plaster herself against him and kiss him, trying to absorb some of that vitality, that charge of energy that radiated from him.

Instead she tossed the towel to him and bent to get another for herself before he guessed her thoughts.

Because in that second of connection she'd read no

sexual intent in Strato's expression. Only the pleasure of someone delighted with what they'd experienced.

As she'd been moments ago. Despite their conversation in the boat, she and Strato had spent a companionable couple of hours exploring sea caves, secret bays and even a sunken wreck. They'd seen more varied sea life than she'd expected and, instead of her amateur companion flagging from exertion and wanting to return to his luxury cruiser, Strato had been as eager as she to investigate further.

It had been fun, far more than she'd anticipated. There'd been no awkwardness or accidentally-on-purpose attempts to crowd her. Nothing sexual.

Not until she turned to see him beside her on the flat rock where they'd left their supplies. Sexual awareness had hit with all the finesse of a tsunami.

She rubbed her fluffy towel briskly over her face, then concentrated on her hair, the bane of her life.

'It must take ages.'

'Sorry?' She looked up from where she was bent over, rubbing her long tresses.

Strato nodded at her hair. 'It must take a long time to dry.'

Cora nodded and straightened, pushing her wet hair behind her shoulders and drying her arms. 'It does. It's a nuisance.'

'But beautiful.' He turned away, leaving her to deal with the silly jolt to her pulse at the compliment. As if she'd never received one before. 'If it's a nuisance, why not cut it?'

He finished using his towel and spread it in the shadow of the white cliff that loomed behind their seaside platform.

Cora looked around for somewhere to lay her own towel while they sat and shared the food they'd brought, but space was small and there was nowhere left but beside Strato's. Telling herself it didn't matter because he'd dropped that sexually charged attitude, she spread her towel next to his.

It made her wonder if perhaps he wasn't as attracted as he made out, that he could turn it off so easily whereas she...

'I promised I wouldn't cut it.' Cora settled on the towel and nodded her thanks as he passed her a water bottle. 'When I was younger Doris was afraid I'd turn into a complete tomboy and made me promise not to cut it. I wasn't good at cooking or sewing, or behaving like a good Greek housewife, all the things she tried to teach me, so it seemed a fair compromise. My father backed her up. Said it reminded him of my mother's long hair.'

That had been enough to convince Cora. Even now, the regret in her dad's eyes whenever she mentioned cutting it short stopped her.

'You're a sentimentalist.'

She looked up but he wasn't watching her. Instead he was hauling the cold bag closer.

Well, she'd wanted him to drop the flirting, hadn't she?

Except she couldn't ignore what he'd said in the boat or the way he made her feel about her body and its increasingly clamorous needs.

'I'm not sure I'd say that.' She paused and took a long draught of blessedly cool water. 'But my father and Doris are special. I care about them.'

Plus there were times, like when Strato complimented her on her hair, that she privately revelled in the flagrantly feminine look. Mostly she was too busy working to think of herself as a sexy woman. Unless she was dealing with sleazy men who thought the generous size of her bust was inversely proportionate to her IQ and that she wanted nothing more from life than to fall into bed with them.

She'd thought she was good at giving them the brush-off. Till Adrian, who'd tricked her.

Cora took another swallow of water, rinsing away the sudden sour taste on her tongue, then handed the bottle to Strato.

His eyes held hers as he lifted it and drank. That now-familiar corkscrewing sensation tightened inside her, drilling down to the aching emptiness within her pelvis. She shifted and looked away, reaching for a tiny tomato and popping it into her mouth.

It burst in a pop of tangy deliciousness and she tried to concentrate on that, not the fact she'd prefer to taste Strato.

He'd taste of salt water and—what was the flavour of that dark golden skin? She imagined licking the line of his sternum, straight up the centre of his chest to his throat. Sucking on that full lower lip.

She gave a shuddery sigh and tried to ignore her tightening nipples.

'More water?' Strato held out the bottle again.

'Not at the moment.' Because putting her lips where his had been seemed too intimate.

'There's wine and beer.'

'I'll stick with water, thanks.' It became clearer by the moment that she needed to keep her wits about her. Lest she give away how aware she was of Strato beside her. It was as if a switch had flicked in her brain, as if the companionable hours they'd spent together meant nothing. Because now her mind filled with him and sex.

Cora passed him a container. 'Chicken wing?' Her thoughts strayed to the day they'd met, with him stretched out, naked and mind-bogglingly attractive, and her offering refreshment. It felt a lifetime ago.

'Thanks.' He took some chicken, biting into it with strong, white teeth.

Cora took some herself and tried to concentrate on the spicy, marinated meat. But the silence crowded around her.

'You've done much snorkelling?' Maybe she could distract herself with conversation.

'Some.' He dropped chicken bones into an empty container, his hairy arm not quite brushing hers, making her quiver.

Cora shot him a sideways glance but he was focused on the aqua and green depths of the sea.

'How about scuba diving?' she asked eventually. 'I know an ideal place. Another wreck, but in deeper water.'

Strato nodded but didn't turn. 'Sounds good to me.'

Yet from this angle he looked to be frowning.

Cora subsided into silence, her usually reliable appetite fading. Her gaze strayed across his broad back to the scar he'd dismissed as the result of an old accident. Curiosity welled but it was fleeting. She wasn't concerned with old scars but with what had gone wrong in the last few minutes.

He was distracted. That wasn't her problem. It wasn't her job to entertain him. Yet the change from enthusiastic companion and would-be seducer, to a man barely aware of her presence, jabbed her ego.

She leaned back on her elbows, looking on the view of their tiny cove. Apart from their small boat there was no sign of people. They were utterly alone.

Strato continued to ignore her. Last night and this morning they'd spoken easily and he'd been a pleasant companion. This afternoon their communication had mainly been via sign language and occasional nods and grins as they swam. Now they didn't communicate at all.

Odd how bereft that made her feel.

Lying back like this, Cora couldn't see his face, except for his cheek and the line of his jaw, which she realised was clenched. It matched the hunched line of his shoulders. She shifted, trying to get comfortable, and noticed the tic of Strato's pulse at his temple. Whatever was on his mind it didn't look like anything relaxing.

Maybe she should head back into the water while he worked off what looked like abstraction or a bad mood. But she'd swum enough. It felt good to relax. Or it would if she didn't increasingly feel tension in the air.

She shifted again. Her flat rock wasn't as flat as she'd thought.

Cora opened her mouth to speak then realised she'd been going to fill the void with chat because Strato's silence felt brooding. But if he had a problem, it wasn't up to her to fix it. He was an adult. Let him deal with whatever bothered him.

Stifling a sigh, she folded her hands behind her head and searched for a comfortable position. That was better—

'If you've finished eating we should go back to the yacht.' His tone was terse.

'The yacht?' She frowned. 'You've barely rested or eaten anything.'

'I'm not hungry and, believe me, I'm not in the mood to rest.' His voice held a rough edge, emerging almost as a growl.

It shouldn't bother her, but his mood tarnished what had been, for her, a lovely couple of hours. Stupid to feel hurt. The illusion of companionship between them, even liking, flickered and faded. Just as well. She wasn't looking for a friendship, or anything else from this man.

Cora rose a little, bracing herself on her elbows. 'What's the problem, Strato? You sound like a bear with a sore head. I thought you liked our swim.'

He nodded but she saw his fist clench at his side, and the tendons stand proud beneath his skin. 'I did.'

Just that. No explanation of why they needed to get back to the yacht. Cora sighed and was about to move to pack up their mini picnic when her obstinate side re-asserted itself. She refused to tiptoe around this man, second-guessing what she'd done to trigger his temper.

'Then what's up? Or am I expected to put up with your sudden mood swings? At least you owe me the courtesy of telling me why you've suddenly turned sour.'

'You don't want to know.'

Cora's breath hissed between her teeth. She did want to know or she wouldn't have asked. But she refused to labour the point. She'd met enough selfish men to waste time with this one. She sat up with a jerk and began jamming their provisions into the bag they'd brought ashore.

In her haste her hand brushed Strato's arm.

He stiffened. His head swung round and her breath jammed back in her throat.

For the man whose gaze pinioned her to the spot wasn't the debonair pleasure seeker she knew, or the charming companion of earlier. There was a fierce light in his eyes while his arched nostrils and tightly drawn mouth hinted at strong emotions.

He looked…elemental. As if spawned from the depths of the ocean or carved from the rock on which they sat. Except he was flesh and blood. She saw the heavy rise of his chest and felt heat radiate from him.

Cora's breath seized and his hot gaze slid down to the rise of her breasts, swelling against the black fabric.

'Cora.' There it was again, that rasping note. A growled warning.

Suddenly she realised she wasn't the only one beleaguered by sexual arousal. It was there in the etched lines of Strato's face and the shimmer of tension between them.

'What don't I want to know, Strato?'

She knew, but she wanted to hear him say it. Because suddenly caution and common sense didn't matter a jot in the face of her compulsion to get close to him.

His mouth twisted in what she might have thought a sneer if she hadn't seen the sweat beading his brow. Strato wasn't bored or moody. He was racked by tension.

'That you're driving me crazy lying there beside me. That we need to return because I promised I wouldn't touch you and I don't break my promises. But I can't take much more.

'Every time you shift I imagine the feel of your bare skin against mine. The slide of our bodies together. The taste of your orgasm in my mouth. The sound of you screaming when I make you come.'

He paused, his breath audible in the thick silence. Cora's own breathing had disintegrated as the visions he conjured stopped her lungs working. Her fingers curled into damp towelling as she clung on tight.

'From the first I've wanted you, Cora. From the very first moment.' His deep voice and frowning face imbued the words with a gravity she felt deep inside. Felt and welcomed because wasn't that how she'd felt too?

'I want to feel your tight heat welcoming me inside. I want to suck your breasts and ravish every inch of your body until you can't remember being with any man but me.'

His massive shoulders rose and fell as he dragged in a slow breath.

'That's why we need to leave.'

Yet he made no move. Maybe he too felt glued to the spot.

Finally she spoke. 'You haven't asked me what I want, Strato.'

His eyes narrowed. 'What do you want, Cora?'

For a second she paused, waiting for her protective instincts to kick in. Obviously they were on holiday, or overwhelmed by the inevitable.

'All of the above.'

She reached for the zip at her throat.

CHAPTER EIGHT

HE'D DIED AND gone to Heaven.

Except Strato didn't believe in Heaven. As he didn't believe in love or fate or anything except the present and what he could see, hear, taste and touch.

His lips curled in a smile so tight it hurt his face. He intended to do a lot of looking, listening, tasting and touching.

He wanted Cora. All of her. In so many ways he'd never be able to satisfy himself today. It would take days, weeks, to work through his fantasies.

His smile widened as he brushed her hand away and took control of that silver loop on her zip.

Good thing he had her for the next month. That would give him time to indulge this gnawing hunger.

He'd planned slow and gentle the first time they were together. Instead he watched his hand tug hard, dragging the zip open with a sibilant hiss, right to the bottom, just above her pubic bone.

Was she bare down there or was there a triangle of dark silky hair over her mound? He wanted to find out. Except gravity distracted him, in the form of her swimsuit parting over her bounteous breasts, a little further with each short, sharp breath.

Strato's gaze fixed there, drawn to those perfect breasts and the way the slick fabric clung to her nipples despite the growing swathe of skin he'd revealed.

He heard a gasp and dragged his attention to her face. Her lips were parted and eyes narrowed in an unmistakably carnal look.

He licked his lips, imagining the taste of her mouth, her breasts, her sex. Her eyes widened and so did the gap between the edges of her zip as her beautiful breasts rose and fell sharply.

Strato knelt astride her, not daring yet to lower himself and lie over her. He might be desperate with want but not so desperate he'd allow this to be over in seconds.

His penis throbbed at the thought of covering her body with his. Instead he lifted his palm to her throat then stroked down and out, pushing the wet fabric aside to uncover one breast, its pert nipple begging for attention.

Strato was a generous man. He liked to please his lovers. Obligingly he lowered his head and fastened his mouth there, shaping her breast with his hand as he drew, gently at first, then harder.

So generous, Doukas! When you've been aching to get your hands and mouth on her breasts from that first day!

She writhed between his knees, hands fastening on his bare shoulders then slipping up to cradle his head. But there was nothing gentle in Cora's touch. She clamped his skull to her as if fearing he might be lunatic enough to pull away.

He smiled against her skin, scented with honey, warm woman and the sea, smoothing the fabric off

her other breast. It was perfect in his hand. Gently he
squeezed as he nipped her flesh and she made a tiny
growling noise in the back of her throat that almost
undid him.

Her patience was as fragile as his.

So he slid his hand down her restless body, past ribs,
navel and soft belly, underneath clingy fabric to downy
hair and a slick cleft that drew his fingers to her core.

Another breathy growl and her pelvis tilted, inviting him in. Strato didn't hesitate. He slid a finger deep,
then two, and felt her grip him. He paused, breathing
hard, reminding himself to wait.

But she couldn't. Her hips rose, her breath coming in
frantic puffs, and he pressed down on her bud, circling
till she jerked beneath him and cried out.

Her rapture went on and on, tempting him to join her.
But he wanted this to last. For his own pleasure, and, he
realised, to imprint on her the fact that he, Strato, was
the lover who could give her such delight. He wanted
her craving his touch. Not once or twice because maybe
it had been a while for her, but because no other man
could give her what he could.

He stilled, stunned by that alien idea. It was almost…
possessive. Nothing he'd experienced before. But he was
too aroused to spare time thinking.

Instead, after one last, luscious lick of her breast, he
drew his hand up her shuddering body, lifted his head
and surveyed his Nereid. Her eyes were closed and her
mouth slack with pleasure.

Good but not good enough. He wanted her eyes fixed
on him, alight with the knowledge it was he, Strato, taking her to the stars.

Gently he moved her arms, helping her out of the

swimsuit, dragging it down her yielding body to bare her ribcage, waist and hips, then all the way down and off.

He'd known she was magnificent. That hourglass figure had snared his attention even covered by baggy shorts and a T-shirt. But knowing and seeing were two different things.

Lightly, not trusting himself to linger lest he get distracted, Strato skimmed his hands over her, following curves and indents. Her waist was narrow and her hips and breasts beautifully symmetrical. And those legs, long and shapely with toned muscle.

He was going to enjoy every moment with his new lover.

He should be crowing at his success, seducing the woman who'd scorned him. But he didn't feel he'd scored a point. Triumphant yes, but with anticipation. He was too aware of his own hungry yearning.

His gaze flicked to the supplies he'd brought and the condoms secreted there. Not yet.

He pushed open her thighs and settled between her legs, inhaling the perfume of sated woman. But not as sated as she was going to be. One hand beneath her rump angled her pelvis and the other reached to tease her breast as he nuzzled her cleft.

Instantly her legs tensed around him. Her eyes shot open, dazzled and unfocused. They glowed a rich golden brown that made him think of treasure. Slowly he licked, long and deep, and found his own treasure.

Cora scrambled up on her elbows, frowning. He licked again, holding her gaze, and he felt her quiver.

'Don't you want—?'

Get up to 4
FREE FABULOUS BOOKS
You Love!

To thank you for being a loyal reader we'd like to send you up to 4 FREE BOOKS, absolutely free.

Just write "YES" on the Loyal Reader Voucher and we'll send you up to 4 Free Books and Free Mystery Gifts, altogether worth over $20, as a way of saying thank you for being a loyal reader.

Try **Harlequin® Desire** books featuring the worlds of the American elite with juicy plot twists, delicious sensuality and intriguing scandal.

Try **Harlequin Presents®** Larger-print books featuring the glamourous lives of royals and billionaires in a world of exotic locations, where passion knows no bounds.

Or **TRY BOTH!**

We are so glad you love the books as much as we do and can't wait to send you great new books.

So don't miss out, return your Loyal Reader Voucher Today!

Pam Powers

'Oh, I want, *Coritsa*. I want all of you. Starting here.'
Holding her gaze, he lowered his mouth.

There it was again, the glimmer of gold between lustrous dark lashes. Her lips were parted, her face flushed with passion and her eyes intent as he stroked her. She looked beautiful and something in his chest swelled.

Her eyelids flickered as he nuzzled, devouring the taste of salt and aroused woman. Her breasts rose, peaked nipples jerking high as he caressed her.

'Strato, I…' Her voice disintegrated on a gasp but the sound of her hoarse voice saying his name was a gift. It echoed in his ears as he took her to the edge. Her toned thighs clamped around his shoulders, her pelvis rising to meet his caresses in a needy rhythm, her heat warming him.

Through it all, his eyes held hers, watching as, by degrees, she slipped closer to—

'Strato!' The waves of her climax broke upon her. He felt it so intimately it was like riding the wave himself. Except his groin, rock hard and aching with need, told him otherwise.

Yet he wouldn't have missed this. Not when her shout became a moan of delight, formed around his name. Not when her dazed eyes held his as if there were nothing else in the world but him.

What was this imperative to mark her as his? To fill her consciousness with him so she didn't think of anyone else?

Later he'd wonder about that. For now, he rose to his knees and reached for protection.

He was so aroused and sensitive that sheathing himself became a test of willpower.

She watched him from slumbrous eyes. That golden-brown stare was a potent aphrodisiac. Her limbs were limp as he settled again between her thighs, gritting his teeth as their bodies touched.

He leaned forward, propping himself on one arm, his erection sliding against slick folds that felt so good he had to focus on his breathing. Guiding himself, he entered, slow, deep and so easy it felt as if they'd done this before.

A flutter of sensation surrounded him, turning into a tight clench that threatened to dissolve his control.

That was when he saw Cora's mouth tilt into a smug smile. As if she liked seeing him on the verge of losing himself.

Most often these days he found his lovers more appealing in anticipation than actuality. Not Cora. Especially when she encircled him with her legs, squeezing him closer to her soft body. Her hands were on his shoulders, fingers digging tight as she urged him to move.

It was exactly what he wanted, to find oblivion in her sweet body. But he wanted more, wanted her enslaved again to an ecstasy she associated only with him.

Slowly Strato moved, withdrawing then thrusting, luxuriating in the feel of them together and the shock in her eyes as he moved to a slow tempo that took every bit of control. If the damned could find Heaven, he almost believed he reached it as he took them both higher.

He'd known they'd be good together but this was…

Thought short-circuited as her hands slid down and gripped his buttocks, urging him higher.

Strato obliged with hard, sharp thrusts that made Cora gasp. Tension rolled through him, tightening his skin, his groin, his whole being, till he knew he had seconds left. Sliding his hand between them, he found her clitoris and circled it hard as he let go and pumped right to her core, again and again and again.

Liquid gold burst around him, melting his brain while his body pounded deep into that luscious body as it convulsed around him. Fire consumed him. Sensations so exquisite they bordered on pain. As he sank into ecstasy it was with the sound of Cora screaming his name.

The sun was noticeably lower in the sky as he spooned behind Cora.

They'd drowsed, limbs tangled, for a long time. Till inevitably he'd needed more and he'd lifted her, tired but delightfully willing, onto his lap and urged her to ride him. Again that powerful rush of ecstasy hit simultaneously. Again it had been phenomenal, like a charge detonating deep in places he was barely aware of any more.

What was it about Cora that made him so needy? Recently his interest in women had waned. Yet with Cora he'd struggled to focus on anything but possessing her from the moment he'd seen her.

The sense of post-coital well-being far surpassed what he'd experienced before.

The novelty of a new lover? That didn't ring true.

She stretched and he watched the sinuous shift of her body, skin gleaming like silk. Cora might have the shape of an earth mother, with lush breasts and hips, but she was slender elsewhere and toned from physical activity.

He slid his palm down her shoulder blade, telling himself not to think about physical activity. Cora was tired. She'd fallen asleep in his arms and he'd been content to hold her, ignoring the hard rock jutting into his hip through his beach towel.

'You're awake.' Her voice was husky with sleep. Had she dreamt about him? About them together?

'I am.' He hadn't slept. He'd lain here, basking in the afterglow, caught up in the profound sense of peace and well-being that was so rare.

He let his hand drift across her back then frowned. 'What's this mark?'

She shrugged. 'Am I bruised? There was a knob of rock under my towel that dug into me.'

Strato feathered his hand across the spot, frowning. 'You should have said. I don't want to hurt you.'

'It's okay. I *wanted* you. It didn't matter.'

He recalled the force of his body slamming into hers, his weight pushing her down, and tasted something metallic on his tongue.

'Even so, I don't want to cause you pain.' He was so much bigger and more powerful. It was why he never set aside all caution, even with the most responsive lovers. The thought of hurting a woman made his blood congeal. 'Next time tell me.'

She shrugged. 'Okay.'

Strato was about to demand she promise but caught himself. Cora would wonder at his insistence. He'd have to be more careful.

Which meant ignoring his libidinous thoughts till they returned to the yacht.

'Are you ready to go back?'

She shot him a look that made his heart thud. The woman was a siren, when even a glance roused him.

As if you weren't already aroused, lying naked against her. Just thinking of her gives you a hard on.

'You don't want to stay here longer?' Her expression and the slide of her body against his sent desire spiralling through him.

But Strato wouldn't be persuaded.

He sat up, ignoring the discomfort in his groin and her challenging pout.

'No. Let's get back. Aren't you looking forward to a hot shower?'

Cora stifled disappointment at his impatience. He'd rather be on his luxury yacht. Despite his getting a buzz out of their snorkelling expedition, she suspected he'd only suggested it to put her at ease, given how reluctantly she'd agreed to this trip.

Strato Doukas was used to a sybaritic lifestyle of indulgence. Not open-air sex on a rock above the sea.

Her throat constricted.

She'd thought it exciting and elemental, that they hadn't been able to resist the magnetism dragging them together.

But maybe for Strato there'd been a feeling of novelty? Something different from sex in luxurious surroundings.

For her the experience had felt life-changing. As if she'd never known rapture till today. He'd definitely enjoyed it too. There'd been no faking that.

Yet for the first time, Cora felt gauche. It was all very well getting swept up by desire, but now, naked with a stranger, especially a stranger used to glamorous, sophisticated women and every sort of luxury...

'Of course. I'll find my swimsuit.'

His arm stretched out over her shoulder, black fabric dangling from his fingertips. A substantial amount of fabric.

For a second she wished she were the sort to wear a topless string bikini. That she were a petite woman who wore mere wisps of material. Then she set her jaw. She'd learned there was no point wishing to be someone she wasn't. Her body was fit and strong. It served her well. She wasn't ashamed of it.

'Thank you.' She plucked the fabric from his fingers and sat up.

'Would you like help?' His voice held a rough edge that sent heat pooling low in her body. Again!

She twisted to look over her shoulder and what she saw made her heart thud against her ribs. Not a bored man thinking of cocktails on the deck. Strato watched her so intently it felt as if he noticed nothing but her. Not the bright sea or vast sky or the little boat that would take them back to his superyacht.

'Scratch that.' His gaze dropped to her bare breasts and he shut his eyes. 'If I touch you we won't get back for hours.'

His words thrilled her. 'Would that matter?'

Strato's eyes snapped open and fixed on hers. Something shifted inside. She told herself it was the aftermath of phenomenal sex. Strato made her previous sensual experience fade into nothing.

'I don't want you getting more bruises because I can't control myself.'

'*That's* why you want to go back?'

He worried about her discomfort? She'd never thought him an ogre but what was one tiny bruise compared with the sexual conflagration they'd shared?

Or maybe what had been so stunning for her was the norm for Strato?

His mouth curved ruefully. 'Well, it's not because I've lost interest. You have a potent effect on me, *Coritsa*.'

Cora struggled and failed to suppress a smile.

This wasn't the sort of relationship she wanted. It was short term and purely physical, yet she enjoyed hearing he found her desirable.

Maybe she'd let Adrian's attitude affect her self-esteem after all. Maybe that was why she responded so avidly to Strato, because he made her feel strong.

'Okay. Give me a minute to get dressed.' Suddenly she noticed how far the sun had moved. She'd had no idea it was so late. 'I promised to call my father this afternoon.' To check on him and that those further hotel bookings had come through.

Cora wriggled into her one-piece, wishing she could do it more gracefully, trying to ignore Strato's gaze on her. When they'd shared their bodies she hadn't minded his flagrantly appraising stare. Yet she wasn't used to being naked with a man, subjected to that intense scrutiny.

'You and your father are close,' Strato murmured. His tone made her wonder about his relationship with his adoptive father.

'He's my dad. There's only been us since I was young.'

Once more that green gaze shimmered with something she couldn't identify. 'Then let's not keep him waiting.'

Strato held out his hand and pulled her up against him. Cora felt that jangle of awareness as their bodies brushed, even though the bones in her legs had jellied from so much pleasure.

His slow smile told her he recognised how she felt. Understanding mixed with smugness and a hint of promise. 'Maybe you should rest when we return. Because I'd like to spend the whole night with you.'

CHAPTER NINE

HE DID. THAT NIGHT and every night after that. And Cora didn't for a moment think of objecting.

What they shared left no room for false pride. Strato might have used outlandish tactics to get her aboard his yacht, but she *wanted* to be here. She wanted him and relished the woman she became with him.

It wasn't that he'd changed her. It was more that with him she was free to be herself as never before. There was no judgement, no expectation.

All Strato demanded was honesty. After her past experiences it had taken her a while to believe that, but it was true. Her honest responses, physically and in conversation, were never dismissed and always welcomed. It made conversations stimulating and love-making unique and special.

In return, Strato was straightforward to the point of bluntness. He had a way of telling her exactly what he'd like to do with her sexually that made her pulse sky-rocket and her body throb in anticipation.

The only exception to his forthrightness was that he rarely spoke of his past and then in only the most general terms, so Cora learned not to raise the subject, respecting his desire for privacy.

She'd moved from her guest stateroom to Strato's vast suite with its enormous bed. It was the most comfortable bed she'd ever slept in. Or maybe it was because she was always exhausted from exertion and pleasure when sleep claimed her.

For a lazy hedonist Strato had so much energy! And not just for sex. Every day they explored, either an island or underwater.

Yesterday it had been a sunken ancient temple, an amazing place she'd never visited. Exploring it with him had felt special. As if they shared something remarkable. Afterwards, as they dined on the deck, and later as Strato gathered her close, Cora had felt herself soften. Not just physically as her body shaped itself to his, but mentally.

Strange as it might once have seemed, she *liked* Strato.

And he…

No, she wouldn't go there, second-guessing his feelings. They were more than halfway through their month together. When the time was up they'd go their separate ways. Strato was an amazing lover but he'd made it clear their relationship was time-limited.

No long-term ties. No happy-ever-after. Those had been his conditions from the first.

Now though, four weeks seemed an incredibly short time. She couldn't imagine going back to her island, or to another research project, and never seeing Strato again.

Cora rolled over and stared at the space beside her, ignoring the dull feeling of disappointment like a lead weight in her middle.

She'd known Strato wasn't still in bed. If he had been

they'd have been touching. Either spooned together or with her sprawled across his chest in what had become one of her favourite positions. Head on his shoulder, arm and knee across him as if to stop him moving away.

They were always touching. Even when they weren't making love. Strato was the most tactile person she'd met. She loved the connection. The brush of his fingers across her arm as they shared some new discovery. The weight of his hand at her breast or waist as he slept.

You'll miss him when you leave.

You miss him now, waking up to find him gone.

What will you be like in eight days' time, knowing you won't see him again?

Cora frowned as she focused on the dented pillow. What would life be like without Strato?

Less exciting. Less pleasurable. Less...warm.

There was something about sharing with him, not just sex, but small things like her joy in a glorious sunset and her weakness for sweet pastries, or big things like her hopes of working permanently in research at a marine reserve. He listened and understood. She had that with her father but there were things she couldn't share with her dad that, to her surprise, were easy to discuss with Strato.

And though he wasn't one to talk about himself, he sometimes told her snippets about his business interests that fascinated her. The complexity of the corporation astounded her, as did the suspicion that he ran it all from aboard his yacht. Clearly he delegated, but there'd been enough video conferences and hours when Strato was shut in his study to convince her that the stories about him as a louche playboy didn't paint the whole picture.

She knew him so well yet there was so much she didn't know. So much she wanted to understand.

Cora pushed back the sheet and swung her legs out of bed. It was early but she wouldn't get back to sleep.

It had been a mistake getting into the habit of falling asleep with Strato. Now it felt wrong, trying to sleep without his solidly muscled body beside her.

She smiled. Maybe she could convince him to come back to bed.

Strato pulled on the handles of the rowing machine, feeling the stretch of muscles in a pleasing rhythm that would, eventually, exhaust him.

Eventually but not soon. He'd woken with Cora spooned against him, her buttocks cushioning his morning erection and his hand at her plump, perfect breast.

He grimaced and pulled harder on the machine, feeling tension rack his shoulders, torso and legs.

He'd been about to wake her for dawn sex as he usually did, when he realised what had begun as a delicious treat had become habit. Each day he woke and reached for her. Not simply because of his almost permanent state of readiness these days, but because he was becoming addicted to giving her pleasure.

Sweat beaded his brow as he worked harder, forcing his body to the limits. As if a gruelling workout could obliterate his craving for Cora.

The desire for sex he could understand. But this was more. He liked being with her. Even arguing some point of disagreement, he felt energised as he hadn't for years. As for pleasing her, physically, or with some treat like the dive yesterday to the temple, he spent more and more time thinking of ways to make her smile.

Strato frowned as he hauled on the handles.

His month with her wasn't turning out as expected. It was becoming complicated.

You don't do complicated, remember? Not in your personal life.

Personal complications equated to emotional engagement.

Strato had devoted the last couple of decades to ensuring he never made the mistake of getting emotionally involved. Because he knew the risks that came with that. The *danger*. He'd vowed that no one else would suffer that danger, that devastation, with him.

'I thought you might be here.'

He halted, heart hammering, as Cora walked barefoot across the gym.

Her hair was pinned up in a haphazard arrangement that made him want to see it spill around her shoulders and back. But it wasn't her hair that snagged his attention. She wore an ultra-short tank top, or perhaps it was a sports bra, and a pair of shorts. Brief shorts that clung. Different from the ones she usually wore. Between the two garments was a swathe of smooth skin and a narrow waist.

His breath slid out in a sigh of approval that snatched in sharply as she bent to drape a towel over a bench near the window. The view from behind dried his mouth. Long, toned legs and tight, perfectly rounded buttocks.

Strato released the handles and the rowing machine stilled.

'What are you doing?'

Good one, Doukas! Asking the obvious is a sure sign you've lost the plot.

'Same as you. Exercise seems a good way to start the

day.' She smiled as she bent into a long, slow stretch, though her eyes didn't meet his. Instantly he wondered why.

Maybe she'd missed him, waking to find him gone. Maybe she wanted him as much as he wanted her.

Yeah, and maybe you've got a one-track mind.

Strato grabbed his towel and rubbed his face, neck and arms.

Cora followed the movement and he felt a spark of excitement.

He pushed aside the notion that had disturbed him only seconds ago—that his involvement with this woman was getting too complex and he needed to pull back. Now he was faced with the reality of her, all his years of pursuing pleasure told him there'd be no pleasure more complete than what he'd experience with her.

He planted his feet on the floor and rose, watching her eyes widen before she turned her head and apparently concentrated on the stretch to her toes.

Strato suppressed a smile. She was supple as well as strong and he appreciated both.

He was always cautious with lovers, given his superior size and power. Yet Cora met him as an equal, revelling in the male strength he always sought to harness. Her size, taller and more robust than most women, though far smaller than him, made it feel as if she were designed specifically to please him, or he her.

That was why sex felt so good. They...matched.

Strato made an executive decision not to pursue that thought further.

Because the implications might make him uncomfortable and he had more pressing concerns.

He slipped his hand into his pocket and found the

condom he'd put there. These days he had them on him at all times. Cora tempted him even in the most prosaic of places, including yesterday on the floor of his walk-in wardrobe.

He'd followed her in there to grab a fresh T-shirt and had accidentally brushed against her, inhaling that intriguing scent of hot, honeyed woman. Abruptly hunger had consumed him. Consumed them. They hadn't made it as far as his bed, mere metres away. Their coupling had been hard and furious, then slow and sweet. Thinking of it made his groin ache and tighten.

'Where are you going to start?' He slung his towel over his shoulder as he approached.

Cora shot him a sideways glance then slowly straightened. When she stood she barely had to tilt her chin to meet his eyes and Strato liked that. He was sick of bending double to kiss a woman.

'Maybe some Pilates work.' She looked around the room. 'I'm not really into weights.'

'No, not weights. Something more holistic, I think.' His thoughts raced ahead and so did his pulse.

'You have a suggestion?' Cora turned, expectation in her expression. Could she read his mind?

'I have. If you'll put yourself in my hands.'

Her gaze dipped to his mouth and, remarkably, Strato felt his chest tighten, his throat constricting. Her eyes met his, shimmering golden brown.

'Why not?' She paused. 'I'm always happy to take advice from an expert.'

She moistened her bottom lip with the tip of her tongue and Strato felt as if she'd swiped that moist tongue across him. She'd done that last night, so effectively he'd shattered far too quickly. He shuddered at the erotic memory.

Sometimes it felt as if *she* was the experienced one, not he, evoking responses so profound they stunned him.

Not because Cora used sexual tricks. It was that, with her, none of this felt stale or second-hand. Everything was fresh and...

Strato sucked in a sharp breath.

Meaningful was the word that came to mind. But that wasn't possible.

There was no hidden meaning here. It was pure sexual chemistry at its best. As he was about to prove.

'Excellent.' He took Cora's hand, his fingers brushing her wrist where her pulse thudded fast. 'Over here.' He drew her to the window beyond which the blue-green sea extended towards the distant mainland.

Strato planted her right hand on the large pane of reinforced glass. Her breath hitched as her eyes caught his in a smoky sideways stare that shot heat to his groin.

'Now what?'

He moved behind her, taking her left hand and planting it on the glass in front of her, then he put his hands on her hips, fingers gripping hard, and tugged her back towards him.

He heard a sigh. Hers or his?

'Comfortable?'

She nodded, then shuffled, hips wriggling, till she came up against him. 'Very.'

Witch! He heard her breathless laugh and grinned. He slid one hand round her hip and down to cup her mound and instantly she pushed into his touch.

'You like that?'

She nodded and when she spoke she sounded breath-less. 'You really think this will give me the workout I need?'

Strato bent forward and nipped the side of her neck. 'Count on it.' His other hand moulded her breast, discovering her nipple already peaked hard. It was one of the things he liked about Cora. She was always as eager for him as he was for her.

She gave another little wriggle of her hips against him and Strato's patience for this game waned. He tucked both thumbs in the waistband of her shorts and dragged them over lush hips and down till they fell at her feet.

His gaze fixed on her bare buttocks, perfect as a peach. 'Now that *is* naughty,' he murmured. 'Not so much as a G-string to preserve your modesty.' He was already shucking his shorts and tearing the condom wrapper.

A gurgle of laughter reached him. 'I didn't think it was my modesty you were interested in.'

She'd be surprised. He loved her naked. But he was almost as aroused seeing her buttoned up, or zipped up, in the case of that wickedly tempting swimsuit.

He slid a palm over the pale globe of her buttock then down between her legs, finally encountering slick folds.

'Aren't you going to take off my top?' Her voice sounded stretched and he could relate. He felt as if his groin were caught in a vice, gripping harder and harder.

'Next time,' he growled as he slid his other hand up her ribcage and under the tight fit of her top. Something like relief engulfed him as her breast filled his hand. That was better. That was what he needed.

'More,' she demanded, pushing into his hands. 'Give me more.'

'I've created a monster,' he teased. 'First you pretend you don't like me and now you're insatiable.'

'You like it. You know you do.'

She was right. Strato couldn't remember delighting in anything more than being with her.

Cora didn't pry or connive for a permanent position in his world. She accepted him as he was. There was no evidence now of hesitation, or of the calculation he'd read in other lovers.

It was as if she didn't give a damn for his money.

Or sense the darkness at the heart of him.

As if that darkness didn't exist.

Strato shivered at the heady illusion.

It had been a long, long time since he'd experienced anything like it.

The powerful realisation tempered his hunger with rare tenderness. He bent his head, feathering kisses across her bare shoulder, trying to slow the surge of need building in his loins.

Her hair tickled him but he couldn't bring himself to let her go long enough to release it. He loved Cora's long tresses, soft and enticing, but not as enticing as her almost naked frame, backing up into his groin, hips circling.

'Stop teasing, Strato!'

He smiled against her skin. This feisty woman really could be imperious. That called to something inside him. As did her sense of humour and her generosity.

'Well, if you're sure you're ready...' He bent his knees and guided himself to her, pausing to give them both a moment to anticipate what was to come. Then with one long, sure thrust he went deep, embedding himself. Her heart pounded beneath his hand and he felt the hot, slick grab of her muscles around him.

For a second they were still, as if the glory of their union took them both by surprise. As if this wasn't simply about two aroused bodies seeking ecstasy but two souls finding each other.

Strato grimaced and let his forehead rest against Cora. He breathed deep and strived for sanity. From the age of eight his life had been firmly rooted in reality. No flights of fancy. No cosy fantasies. No sentiment.

So when Cora angled her body, pushing back against him, hips circling needily, Strato shoved aside the outlandish thoughts and set about giving her what she wanted.

First with his hand between her thighs, till she trembled and cried out, her inner muscles convulsively clutching him. Then, when her sighs had died, unleashing his own need, powering fast and hard till the view of sea and sky blurred and exquisite sensation filled him.

On the cusp of losing himself, he knew a moment's hesitation, an atavistic warning that this was something other than simple sex.

Then it was too late and Strato lost himself in bliss and Cora's welcoming body.

Later, when finally they could make their bodies move, he carried her to the spa on his private deck. She slumped in his arms, her head tucked beneath his chin as he stared out at another magnificent new day.

Occasionally she snuggled closer, nuzzling his throat or shifting her weight on his thighs, and heat drenched him. Not heat from the spa or even residual heat from sex, but something deep in his gut.

Strato frowned. They had just over a week left together yet he was no nearer being ready to let her go.
With any other partner he'd be impatient to end their
liaison.

Why not now?

'That's what I meant to ask you. You keep distract-
ing me and I keep forgetting.' Cora moved as if to draw
back from him, probably so she could meet his eyes,
but he tightened his embrace. He was comfortable like
this, enfolding her against him.

'What did you forget?'

'Something my father said.'

'Is there a problem with the hotel bookings?' According to his information, that had gone smoothly. The boat
chartered to take guests from the mainland and back
had even become the unofficial public ferry for the island while the government-funded one was repaired.

'No. That's fine. Everyone's busier than ever with
all these guests. The businesses along the harbour are
reporting increased income too.'

'So?' He slid a finger up her throat and around the
back of her ear where she was particularly sensitive and
was rewarded with a quiver of response.

'Do you know an organisation called Asteri?'

Strato stilled. 'Why do you ask?'

'The bulk of the bookings are from your company,
but my father mentioned someone from a place called
Asteri also reserved quite a few rooms.'

'So?'

Once again Cora shifted as if to look up at him, but
he held her where she was.

'I wondered if that's you too, under a different name.'

And there he'd been, congratulating himself on the fact that Cora didn't pry.

Strato chose his words carefully. 'I don't own a company called Asteri.' He paused, seeking a change of subject to distract her. 'Surely you and your father are happy to have bookings from a range of places.'

'Oh, we are. And now there's transport to the island again, we've had more private bookings. The season is looking to be our best ever. Thank you, Strato.' She turned to plant a kiss at his collarbone.

'You're welcome.'

He didn't refer to the fact that was the only reason Cora was here, because he'd presented her with a deal too good to refuse.

As for the question about Asteri, it wouldn't be disastrous if she learned about his involvement. Except it was something Strato kept strictly private. Only a very trusted few knew of his links to the organisation.

Because it was the one thing in his life that he felt strongly about. Even building his uncle's company into a mega-successful corporation wasn't as important as Asteri.

If the press became aware of his involvement, there'd be endless curiosity and possibly someone, finally, would dig up the past he preferred to forget.

'Strato? Are you okay?' Brandy-coloured eyes held his and it felt, remarkably, as if it wasn't a throwaway question. It felt as if Cora really was concerned. As if she tried to see deep inside him.

'Never better, *Coritsa*.' Deliberately he brushed his hand over her bare breasts and watched her shiver. Yet still her gaze held his.

The potency of that look, and of his yearning response, hit him like a blow. Almost as if he wanted to share things with Cora that he'd never shared with a soul, not even his well-meaning aunt or the experts who'd probed him.

His breath jammed and backed up in his cramping lungs.

He refused to go there. Not ever again. It was unthinkable.

Which meant something had to change. He'd created a hothouse atmosphere, alone on the yacht with Cora. That was why he was plagued by unfamiliar thoughts about sex becoming something more. And about unburdening himself.

They needed a distraction. Then Cora wouldn't have time for curiosity.

Strato slid his hand past her soft belly to the curls between her legs. She gasped, thighs opening instantly for him, and he smiled his approval.

He *did* like this woman. So much.

But he couldn't afford to let her upset his well-ordered life or unleash old hurts.

'Remind me to tell you later about the surprise I have for you.' Then, before she could question him, he took her mouth and seduced her all over again.

CHAPTER TEN

CORA INHALED THE scent of sea and flowering geraniums. The latter were a burst of bright red in painted olive-oil tins clustered against the last whitewashed house in the village.

'I like your surprise.' The tiny harbour and bright fishing vessels, the sunlight dancing off clear water and the joy of walking hand in hand with Strato made a perfect end to the day. 'I've never been here.'

Strato's gaze caught hers and heat danced inside. 'I'm glad to bring you somewhere new. But this is just a stop-off. The surprise is tomorrow—'

A cry wafted on the late afternoon breeze. A seabird? Cora turned but saw nothing. It was Strato who spotted it, a bundle of colour at the bottom of the steps to the harbour.

Before Cora had even taken it in, Strato loped across and vaulted off the stone wall.

When Cora caught up she discovered the bundle was a child. A little boy with huge, overbright eyes and two badly skinned knees, red with blood. Beside him a girl, a little older, scolded him for jumping off the steps. 'I told you not to. You're not big enough yet.' Despite her words, she was clearly upset and Cora guessed both children had had a nasty fright.

Strato squatted before them, introducing himself and discovering the siblings were Costa and Christina. He was friendly, but matter-of-fact, and Cora sensed his attitude stopped a flood of tears. He asked Costa if he could stand.

The boy did, but winced with pain.

'I'm all right,' he said, blinking hard.

'I can see that,' Strato responded, checking he had no other injuries. 'But it might be hard climbing the steps.'

The girl twisted her hands. 'I'll have to call Mamma. I said we'd play outside while she fed the baby but—'

'We don't need to bother your mother yet,' Strato said as Cora opened her mouth to say the same. They shared a look and again she experienced that sense of connection as if they read each other's thoughts. It happened more and more frequently.

'We could help you up the stairs,' she said. 'I'm Cora and my friend Strato is very strong. He could carry Costa.'

'I'm not a baby!' That dried the boy's tears.

'Of course not,' Strato said, 'but it's sensible to accept help when you need it. Cora and I are going to buy ice cream, if there's somewhere that sells it.'

'There is.' Costa looked suddenly eager. 'I could show you.'

'Costa! We can't. Mamma—'

'Maybe,' Strato said, 'you could ask your mother if it's all right. If you show us the way, I'd be grateful. Perhaps you'd both like ice cream as a thank you?'

Minutes later, after Christina had dashed into the house with the geraniums and checked with her mother, the four proceeded to the village store. Christina walked beside Cora, asking where they came from and whether they liked the island. Costa, on Strato's shoulders, grinned and shouted all the things he could see from so high.

By the time they settled down with their ice creams, Costa allowed Strato, rather than Cora, to tend to his scrapes and both children chattered about their island, the fine church, the huge underground cavern and the bay where legend said a local boy once rode dolphins.

The interlude revealed a new side to Strato. His patience and good humour with the children intrigued Cora. But she'd already known he wasn't just the careless playboy he made out. He'd shown genuine concern and an appreciation not only of Costa's pride, but of Christina's need to check in with her mother for permission. His patience, thoughtfulness and unflappable attitude were typical of the man she'd begun to know.

'What are you thinking about?' Strato asked as they walked alone to the tender that would take them to his vessel.

'You with those children. I never imagined you with kids.'

His smile stiffened. 'You imagined right. I don't intend to have any.'

There it was again, that blare of warning. The same as when he'd said he'd never settle down with a family.

'But you understand them. You're used to being around kids.'

'Not at all.' When he read her curious look, he sighed and finally added, 'I had siblings, one older and one younger. I remember what it was like, being with them.'

His voice dipped and Cora felt the gravity of his words. That was when they sank in.

He'd *had* siblings. Past tense.

Her pulse throbbed. The articles she'd read implied he was an only child. Had they died before or after he was adopted?

She couldn't ask. Not when it was clear he didn't want to discuss it.

Silently Cora tucked her hand in his. She felt privileged he'd shared so much when she knew he disliked talking about his past. Maybe one day he'd share more. The fact he'd told her this was surely proof of their growing trust.

But though she didn't ask, her thoughts raced. Was that why he didn't want a family? Because he'd experienced loss early in life? Was he scared to love and lose again?

Where Strato was concerned, her curiosity was boundless.

Cora had approached Athens by sea multiple times. Usually by ferry or occasionally a research vessel. This time, instead of landing at the public dock, she was at a private marina of luxury boats.

For the first time in weeks she felt out of her comfort zone. What was she doing in a place like this?

Amazing how swiftly she'd acclimatised to Strato's superyacht. Not just the yacht, but him. It felt natural to wake in his arms then spend all day and night with him.

A shiver skated down her spine despite the sunshine. She resented coming into Greece's capital, because it meant less time solely with Strato.

When had he become so important that the prospect of being surrounded by others, not having him to herself, bothered her?

She told herself it was the stupendous sex, a revelation to a woman who hadn't realised how deep her own carnal appetites ran. Strato awakened a sexually confident woman she'd initially found hard to recognise.

Yet Cora felt more than physical desire. She liked the man, and had developed an intimacy with him plus a level of trust she'd never known before.

Maybe it was as well they were in Athens. Time alone with Strato messed with her mind.

'There you are, *Coritsa.*' Warm arms wrapped around her and she felt his hard frame at her back. She inhaled Strato's spicy scent and something in her eased. She let her head drop back against his shoulder. 'Ready to go ashore?'

She nodded, telling herself Athens would be a nice change. A shame she didn't believe that.

'Excellent. I've got business to attend to but you'll find lots to keep you amused. Then tonight we're invited to a private dinner.'

Cora froze. They weren't spending the day together? She'd imagined…

That Strato would spend the day visiting crowded tourist sites with her? Or sit in a simple *taverna* with her when his onboard chef produced the most amazing meals every day?

Of course he had people to see, a reason for coming here. If she'd been thinking she'd have organised to catch up with old colleagues. It might still be possible, even at short notice.

Yet bitter disappointment lingered on her tongue. She turned. 'A private dinner? Where?'

'A business contact. Damen Nicolaides. He and his wife, Stephanie, are having a dinner at their Athens home.'

'Damen Nicolaides, the shipping magnate?'

'You've heard of him?'

Heard of him? He was more famous than the prime minister. Like Strato, his name was synonymous with wealth.

'I know of him.'

Cora breathed deep. Dinner with a couple of world-famous billionaires instead of just one. Strange how daunting that seemed.

Suddenly she realised how little she'd really seen of Strato's life. There was another side to his world about which she knew nothing. What a novelty she must be to him. A change from the usual sophisticated socialites.

'Are you okay?' His rough voice scraped her skin.

Cora swallowed, shoving aside the idea that that was really why Strato wanted her. Because she was a change from the usual. But it was true. She'd let herself forget she and Strato came from separate worlds.

'Of course. What are our plans?'

For a moment longer he stared deep into her eyes but Cora was prepared now, drawing on the protective reserve she hadn't needed in weeks.

'We'll go to the Nicolaides home first as that's where my meeting is. That way you can meet them before dinner tonight. I know dinner with complete strangers can be daunting.' He stroked his hand down her cheek in a gesture that made her heart squeeze. That, and his intent gaze, made it feel as if he was genuinely concerned about her. 'We'll meet on board around five. There'll be time to…relax before we leave for dinner.' His mouth curled in a familiar smile that spoke of sex and Cora's blood heated to flashpoint.

Just like that!

Even knowing she was only with Strato as a temporary diversion.

You can't complain. You're revelling in it. You're using Strato for your own pleasure as much as he's using you.

Yet the thought of their month ending and them going their separate ways loomed like a dark cloud on the horizon. A disaster she didn't want to think about.

'Sounds good. I have plenty to keep me busy.'

Like buying something to wear tonight. In a fit of pique at being manoeuvred aboard Strato's yacht, she'd packed only casual clothes, mainly shorts and T-shirts. Nothing for dinner with a bunch of billionaires. Pride dictated she find something better than the olive-green capri pants and cream top she wore now, even though she knew she couldn't compete with the other guests' designer clothes.

'That reminds me. I have something for you.'

Strato fished out a credit card.

Cora stiffened. She flashed a killing look into those enigmatic green eyes. 'I don't need your money.' Her tastes were simple and she had no intention of spending a fortune.

His dark brows rose. 'I know women, Cora. You'll feel out of place tonight unless you wear something sophisticated like the others. I don't want you feeling uncomfortable. You're only attending to keep me company, so I'll buy the new outfit.'

She was torn between indignation at his *I know women*, as if she were the same as all his other lovers, and something far softer at his consideration. He knew he put her in a difficult position and tried to make things easier.

Then don't force me to go somewhere I'm not comfortable!

But she couldn't say that. He had a right to meet friends and associates. She was a competent woman, able to hold her own amongst strangers, even ones born with silver spoons in their mouths.

'Thanks for the thought, but I'll manage. I don't want your money.' It felt like being bought.

Which might have made sense if she hadn't accepted his deal to fill her father's hotel with paying guests. Was that why she felt so outraged? Was she trying, belatedly, to salvage self-respect?

Strato stared down at her. 'Don't let pride stop common sense. Buy something for tonight.'

'Absolutely not.'

'Damn it, Cora. I'm not trying to buy your soul, just make tonight easier!'

Before she could stop him he shoved the card in the tiny pocket of her top and took her arm, turning her towards the gangplank.

One glance showed his jaw set like granite. But his tension didn't ameliorate hers. She wanted to rip out his credit card and toss it in the harbour. Except that would be childish. She'd simply use her own money and return the card, untouched, at the end of the day.

Yet her temper simmered all the way to the Nicolaides' estate. Possibly because Strato remained tight-lipped too. Gone were the charming smiles and the camaraderie, much less intimacy.

Was he so used to getting his own way that he got in a temper when crossed?

She wrapped her arms around herself. Clearly she didn't know him as well as she'd thought. All she knew was the side he let her see. The carefree, sexy man who was surprisingly thoughtful and great company. But he maintained definite barriers. He erected one whenever his family was mentioned. He'd shoved up another now, when she refused to do as he ordered.

Her mood worsened as she watched the city go by while Strato devoted himself to his phone as if she didn't exist.

It was a long time since she'd thought of Strato as like Adrian. Now she wondered if she was mistaken and Strato was just as egocentric. He hadn't seemed so before, but she'd been in such a haze of well-being...

When they arrived at a gated property with lush gardens and a winding drive that led, finally, to a breath-stealing mansion, Cora's heart dived. She could just about face this with Strato's support. Right now, though, his expression was cool.

Great! She breathed deep and moved towards the huge bronze front door that swung open at their approach.

Now she felt Strato's hand at her elbow and some of her nerves eased.

He was still miffed. She felt the tension in his tall body. But he was perfectly polite to the housekeeper who showed them into a stunning sitting room of ivory and gold with black accent pieces.

'Mr Nicolaides will be with you shortly. Please make yourself comfortable here or on the terrace.' Then, with a promise of refreshments, the woman bustled out.

Strato's hand dropped and with it Cora's heart.

Was she so dependent on his approval? The idea shocked her. She'd never been dependent on a man. It worried her.

Instinctively Cora moved towards the wide terrace with its spectacular view over the city to the sea.

'Wait, Cora! We need to talk.' She turned and Strato's expression made her pulse leap. He didn't look angry now. She thought she saw her own longing reflected there.

Then his phone rang. He pulled it out and glared at the screen, swearing under his breath.

'It's okay. Take the call.' She'd gathered from his calls in the car that today's business was important.

'But *then* we talk. It's important.'

Cora wasn't sure if it was an order or a promise but she nodded. She was unsettled by the way their harmony had fractured, but it seemed Strato wanted to put that behind them too.

She strolled along the paved area, towards a magnificent azure pool fringed with brightly blooming shrubs. A taller shade tree beckoned and she approached it, admiring the setting.

'Damen, you should have asked me first.' From above came a woman's voice. 'I'm happy to invite Strato to dinner. But to have to entertain one of his bimbos today! How could you? I had other plans for this afternoon.'

Cora froze as she realised the woman was talking about *her*. One of Strato's bimbos.

Ice crackled along her veins and into her bones. Her stomach hollowed.

She saw someone move on a balcony above and swiftly turned away, plunging deeper into the garden.

Stupid to feel hurt. Yet the words caught her on the raw, like pressure on a bruise, after what had happened this morning. She was Strato's woman, but only temporarily. That didn't make her a bimbo, but she didn't like to think what it *did* make her.

She wasn't wanted here. She felt her skin crawl, knowing she was an unwanted guest. She'd leave as soon as she could. But first she had to face her reluctant hosts.

Eventually she forced herself to return to the house.

Cora found a couple talking to Strato, a handsome man who smiled and introduced himself as Damen and his petite wife, Stephanie, who looked at her gravely and offered a fleeting smile, her hand on her baby bump.

For ten minutes they chatted. Then Damen invited Strato to his study to discuss business.

Yet Strato lingered, surveying Cora as if he sensed her distress. Instead of following Damen he moved towards her and she had the horrible feeling he'd ask if she was okay. Which she wasn't. Her emotions were too close to the surface. From his frown she guessed he thought it was because of their spat earlier.

Cora pinned on a smile that felt too tight. 'Enjoy your discussions. I'll think of you stuck inside while I'm out in the sunshine.'

Strato stopped before her, his gaze searching. Then he pulled her up into his arms and kissed her soundly on the mouth. Her knees softened as she clutched him needily.

'I'm sorry about earlier,' he murmured against her ear. 'I acted like a fool. Forgive me?'

Stunned, she pulled back and nodded. The apology

was unexpected. She'd assumed he was too used to getting his way to see her side.

'We *will* talk later.' He paused. '*Are* you okay?'

'I am.' Now her smile was real. 'Go and do your business.'

Strato kissed her again. Then with a lingering, molten look that singed several vital organs, he followed their host.

Wiping her hands down her capri pants, Cora swallowed. She turned to her hostess. Damen had invited her to spend the afternoon with Stephanie, saying his wife was looking forward to the company, but Cora wouldn't stay where she wasn't wanted. 'Thanks for the invitation to stay, but I—'

'No! Please!' The other woman looked horrified. 'Not before—'

'It's okay, really. I need to—'

'Please!' Stephanie shot to her feet and actually wrung her hands. 'Not before I apologise.' She breathed deep and colour washed her cheeks. 'I was dreadfully rude. What I said on the balcony... I felt about an inch tall when I realised you'd heard me.'

Cora bit her lip, feeling incredibly uncomfortable. 'You weren't to know I was there.'

'It was ungenerous of me. For what it's worth, I see that I was wrong. You're not what I expected.' She shook her head. 'I was upset and the thought of being stuck all afternoon trying to make conversation with a...'

'Bimbo?'

Her face turned grave again and Cora realised it wasn't disapproval making her look that way but embarrassment.

'I'm so sorry. That will teach me to control my temper.' Her mouth wobbled and suddenly Cora felt sorry for her.

'Maybe you should sit down, Stephanie.'

'Steph, please.' She sighed and subsided onto a lounge. 'Please, take a seat.' She waited till Cora did before speaking again, smiling ruefully. 'You sound like Damen. He's always telling me to put my feet up.'

'It's nice that he's concerned for your health.'

'It is, but he's smothering me! He keeps finding reasons to stay at home with me.' Her eyes glowed and her smile grew. 'There are *definite* benefits to having Damen being attentive. But he tries to stop me going out alone. Says I do too much and I should be resting when I'm perfectly healthy and full of energy.'

Cora tried to imagine what it would be like having a loving partner hovering, looking after you that way.

It wouldn't be a man like Strato, since he didn't believe in long-term relationships. She repressed a sigh.

'So I'm afraid when he asked me to stay and keep you company I lashed out. I thought he suggested it to keep me in when I'd planned to go out.'

'You can still go. I have to do some shopping myself.'

'You do?' Steph sat forward. 'Maybe we could go together.' She frowned. 'Although I'll understand if you don't want to. After the dreadful thing I said...'

'Stop it! You're beating yourself up over nothing.' It was true. Hearing the other woman's explanation, Cora knew she'd be foolish to take offence at her earlier words.

Steph's eyes widened and Cora spread her hands. 'Sorry. I have a habit of saying what I think.'

There was a gurgle of laughter. 'So do I. You have no idea how often I have to bite my tongue.'

Cora felt a smile pull her mouth wide. 'I suspect I have some idea.'

'Seriously, feel free to do your shopping alone,' Steph said. 'But if you'd like company, I know my way around Athens, even if I am a foreigner. If you tell me what you're looking for I might have suggestions.'

'Something to wear tonight. I didn't bring any dresses. Just shorts and trousers.'

Steph's eyes gleamed. 'I know a couple of places. I could show you.'

Cora eyed the gorgeous aqua dress the other woman wore. It looked simple but even she knew such simplicity came at a high cost.

'I'd like that. There's just one thing.' She lifted her chin. 'I'm on a budget.' At Steph's steady look she continued. 'I pay for my own clothes and I'm a currently-out-of-work biologist.'

Steph grinned. 'You *really* aren't what I expected. No wonder Strato is smitten.' Her words rocked Cora. Strato? Smitten? 'I think I know the place to find what you're after.' She shot to her feet. 'Shall we go?'

It turned into a lovely day. Steph was funny, friendly and so down-to-earth Cora found herself relaxing. It helped to learn the vast Nicolaides wealth was new to Steph and that she was still coming to grips with it, though she was overwhelmingly happy with her adoring husband.

They went to a boutique in an upmarket area that looked alarmingly expensive, but Steph said there might be bargains to be had. Typically, there wasn't much in the store in Cora's size, but instead of waving them goodbye, the saleswoman asked them to come back in an hour.

They filled in the time lunching and talking non-stop. They were laughing as they returned to find the saleswoman beaming. Two dresses had been procured especially for Cora and she was ushered straight into the change room where she stopped, staring.

'I'm afraid they're not quite what I had in mind.'

'You don't like them?' The saleswoman's eyebrows shot up. 'The colours are perfect for you.'

Cora shook her head. The bronze silk with its narrow shoulder straps and flirty skirt was so gorgeous she almost feared to touch it. The vibrant red with the plunging neckline and slim fit would turn her into someone sophisticated and sexually confident. Someone who could turn any man's head.

'It's not that. They're beautiful. But the price…' There was no price tag on either but they were obviously out of her range.

The saleswoman smiled. 'Mrs Nicolaides said you need something for her dinner tonight. She's a very good customer so there is a substantial discount. Plus, if anyone were to ask where you got your dress…' She shrugged. 'Word of mouth is better than paid advertising.'

In the end Cora couldn't resist. Both were amazing. She felt glamorous and confident in a way she never did in her usual little black dress. When the saleswoman produced mid-height strappy sandals to match each dress, Cora had a rush of blood to her head, buying both outfits.

Fortunately, with the hotel making a profit, her father had transferred money into her account in lieu of the wages she hadn't drawn in months.

From there she and Steph searched for curtain fabric

for Steph's nursery. Then had foot massages and pedicures. After that it was nearly five and the traffic was manic. Steph suggested Cora get ready at her house, instead of trekking to the port and back. It seemed sensible and Cora had time to soak in a scented bath before facing the dinner with a bunch of privileged strangers. Though, if they were like Damen and Steph, it wouldn't be so bad.

And Strato would be there. Her pulse accelerated as she thought of him and that wonderful, mind-melting kiss.

She'd missed him when she took the logical option to return to the Nicolaides house rather than the yacht. She'd rather have bathed with him, even if it meant a rush to get ready because they'd been busy doing more interesting things than dress for dinner.

Cora smoothed her hands down her dress. She'd spent ages getting ready, not wanting to look out of place amongst his friends and acquaintances. But mainly because she wanted Strato to look at her in admiration.

You want him to look at you the way Damen looks at Steph. Not just with sex on his mind but as if you're the one and only woman in the world for him.

Horrified, Cora bit her lip.

She couldn't be so naïve.

Yet as Cora took one final survey of her reflection, she avoided her eyes in the mirror. Because she feared what she might see.

CHAPTER ELEVEN

Strato paced the sitting room. He'd arrived early and Damen and Stephanie weren't down. Nor was Cora and, short of knocking on every door in this vast place, there was no way of finding her.

His discussions with Damen had gone successfully yet he'd found it difficult to concentrate.

That argument on the yacht and Cora's obstinacy over a little thing like buying a dress! He'd been trying to protect her from a potentially uncomfortable position.

The women tonight would be dressed expensively and he didn't want them looking down their noses at Cora. She was worth a dozen of them. He'd dragged her into this world. It was up to him to look after her.

Strato paused mid-stride. Was that why he was agitated? He wanted to look after Cora?

He breathed deep, controlling a ripple of unease.

It was a long, long time since he'd tried to look after anyone. Tried and failed abysmally.

His gut clenched so viciously it was like a hammer blow.

He set his jaw and yanked his thoughts to the present. This was different. He was doing the right thing by his current lover. Despite what the press said, he had at least a thread of decency in him. His mouth quirked cynically.

Cora was proud and independent yet it irked him that she didn't trust him enough to accept his help without argument. She trusted him with her body. Why fuss over a credit card?

Other women would happily spend his money.

Maybe that was why he was restive. He wasn't used to unpredictability. Cora hadn't returned to him at the yacht. When Damen said the women were late and Cora would get ready at the house, Strato had wanted to demand she meet him. Except he didn't have her phone number! He refused to use Damen as a go-between, passing a message via his wife.

Strato had felt powerless and he didn't like it.

A sound made him turn and he lost his train of thought.

'Cora.' His voice was so thick her name sounded unfamiliar.

She stood in the doorway and for the life of him Strato couldn't move. His feet were soldered to the floor, his tongue stuck to the roof of his mouth.

He knew her body intimately. He ran his fingers through her long hair daily and never tired of watching expressions chase across her lovely face. Yet she surprised him.

Her olive skin glowed and her hair was a gleaming curtain over one shoulder. She'd done something that made her eyes smoky and her lips…her parted lips made him want to devour her.

That dark red dress accentuated every dip and curve. The V neck plunged deep but not outrageously. The fabric clung to breasts and hips but flowed freely around her as she shifted her weight on pretty shoes that gave her added height.

His stasis broke and he strode closer. He hungered for her lush body, her mouth…

'Strato.' She sounded breathless.

Good. He'd hate to think he was the only one.

But when he wrapped his arms around her, she put her palm to his chest and glanced over her shoulder.

'Someone's coming.'

'And I should care because…?' He lowered his head.

Her smile sent relief shooting into his bloodstream. He'd missed her. He hadn't liked it that they'd parted without properly resolving their argument.

Though, looking at her ravishing form, he could see she'd clearly accepted his help. That outfit was worth every penny of its no doubt exorbitant cost.

Before he could kiss her she whispered in his ear. 'I'm nervous enough. I'd rather not meet the others wearing smudged lipstick.'

Strato didn't care what others thought. He didn't care about her lipstick. She should be thankful he didn't pick her up and take her straight back to the yacht. Yet he stopped.

He closed his eyes, breathing deep. Her delicate scent wafted to him and he pressed his mouth to her neck, nibbling and kissing. Cora sighed and arched in his hold, grabbing his biceps as if afraid she'd fall.

Now Strato felt better. Now he held Cora close and felt her eager, yielding body.

Crazy that he'd wondered if she'd had enough of him. That she'd rather browse the shops than be with him.

His plan to bring her to the city where there'd be

distractions had been madness. He wanted her completely to himself.

'Strato. What do you think of Cora's dress?' He lifted his head to see Stephanie enter on her husband's arm. She wore a mischievous smile.

Reluctantly he straightened and turned, holding Cora to his side. The silky material beneath his hand slipped across firm, rounded flesh and he swallowed hard.

'Beautiful. Almost as exquisite as the woman wearing it.' He felt Cora start as if he'd surprised her.

How could that be? She knew he was fascinated by her body. So much so that he contemplated negotiating an extension of their time together. Though he suspected little negotiation was necessary. The way she leaned against him suggested she'd be as eager as he.

Belatedly he focused on his hostess. 'I'm lucky to be in the company of two such gorgeous and clever women.'

Stephanie's grin widened and Damen made a smiling comment about not trying to sweet-talk his wife.

If Strato weren't so eager to have Cora to himself he'd have enjoyed an evening in their company. He respected Damen's business acumen and liked him and his wife. But soon they were joined by more guests.

The evening didn't go as Strato had envisaged.

He'd imagined being in company would lessen his preoccupation with Cora. The opposite was true. The guests were pleasant, witty and well informed but he wasn't interested. Not when, for the first time, he felt jealous.

It took a while to realise what it was. That sour tang of annoyance, that tightening of his shoulders whenever the art collector across the table looked at Cora as if he'd like to add her to his private gallery. Or the young archaeologist, who shared her passion for scuba diving, kept trying to monopolise her.

Strato told himself it didn't matter. She'd go home with him. Yet he prickled with discomfort when she smiled at another man, or got absorbed in what they had to say.

Possessiveness was unprecedented. Never had he cared enough about any woman to feel jealous.

It was illogical. Yet he couldn't conquer it. Could only weather it and warn off her admirers with glares and blatant signals that Cora was *his*.

Strato's consolation was the way she leaned close to him. And the tremor he felt run through her when he stroked her leg beneath the table. And her smiles, that promised so much.

So he endured it. He talked with the other guests, ate his meal, and complimented their hosts on a pleasant evening. But at the first chance after dinner he pushed back his chair.

'I'm afraid you'll have to excuse us. It's time we left.'

'Left?' The art collector frowned. 'But it's early.'

Cora turned, a question in her eyes. He held her gaze, his mind full of the things they'd do when they got back to the yacht. Colour flushed her cheeks.

'We're sailing tonight.'

'Tonight?' That was Damen. 'But you just arrived today.'

'It was a flying visit.'

'But surely—'

Cora moved her chair back. 'You're right. We don't want to miss the tide.' As if that mattered. She turned to their hosts. 'Thank you so much, I've had a lovely evening.'

Strato took her hand and felt the pulse at her wrist jump. Was she wound as tight with need as he?

The goodbyes took too long, but he contained his impatience, again thanking Damen and Stephanie, and watching as the two women said fond farewells. He wasn't sure what he'd expected, bringing Cora here, but she'd been unhappy earlier and it was good to see she'd bonded with the other woman.

Finally, as his patience reached its limit, they were on their way. Strato folded his arms across his chest, took a deep, shuddering breath and released it.

'What's wrong?' Cora looked from the soundproof glass separating them from the driver to Strato, who avoided her gaze. What had happened to the man whose molten stare had promised passion ten minutes ago?

'Nothing.'

'Strato, I can *feel* the tension radiating from you.'

Finally he turned his head, and she saw in the passing streetlights that his face was set.

He breathed deep, his chest and crossed arms rising. 'What's wrong? Apart from the fact I had to sit for hours while every man there ate you up with his eyes?'

Cora's heart leapt in disbelief. Strato was jealous?

She'd wondered if their relationship was morphing into something new, but told herself that was because her feelings for him were changing. She'd never expected his to alter. Strato had made it clear, and reiterated often, that he didn't want anything long term.

'I wasn't attracted to any of them.' There was no need to tell him that. Yet it felt important to make that clear.

'I enjoyed the conversation and the interesting company but the only man I want to spend the night with is you.'

'I'm glad to hear it.'

He took another breath, yet kept his arms folded.

Cora frowned. '*You* were the one I let touch me under the table.' She'd done some touching too, her hand straying to the rock-hard muscle of his thigh. She'd revelled in his twitch of response. 'It's ridiculous to get grumpy about men looking at me.'

She refused to apologise for having a good time. Even if the best part had been seeing Strato's stunned reaction to her appearance. That had given her confidence, and a thrill, feeling her feminine power so blatantly.

'There's no need to sit with your arms crossed and your jaw clenched as if I've done something wrong.'

'You think that's what I'm doing?'

'What else? You're keeping your distance.'

She'd grown accustomed to his touch and missed it now, especially after the way he'd looked at her earlier.

Abruptly he laughed, the husky sound curling around her in the darkness. 'I'm sitting like this, *Coritsa*, because I'm trying, very hard, to resist ravishing you in the back seat of this limo.'

Cora's eyes widened and heat speared deep into her pelvis. 'Oh!'

'Yes, oh. I might have a reputation as a profligate but I refuse to strip that delectable dress off you in full view of our driver or anyone on the street.'

Cora opened her mouth to say he could ravish her without stripping her naked, then thought better of it.

'I like that you're tempted, but I think I'd rather wait till we have privacy.'

'My thoughts exactly.' His voice dropped to a growling rumble that did devastating things to her.

No man had affected her as profoundly or as easily as Strato. Not even the man she'd once believed herself falling in love with.

The difference between him and Strato, whose muscles bunched as he fought not to touch her, couldn't be greater. How had she thought them similar?

On impulse, she wanted to tell Strato how much that meant. He'd done so much for her. Not just saving her father's hotel. Or giving her the holiday of a lifetime, or even the most wonderful sexual pleasure. He'd helped heal wounds that had festered too long. He'd given her back her confidence as a woman, her sense of her own power, and, most surprisingly, her ability to trust.

She'd been so busy cutting herself off from her past, she hadn't given herself permission to process what had happened or move on from it. Instead she'd pushed it into a locked box labelled 'Adrian' and tried not to think of it.

Cora swivelled on the seat to look directly at Strato. 'There's something I like even more than your passion.' She paused, feeling as if she crossed a bridge with this confession, but feeling she owed it. 'That's your honesty.'

'Because I admit I want to have wild, unrestrained sex with you in the back of a moving vehicle?' His voice was harsh as if he really suffered from the effort of holding back. In the gloom she caught the glint of his eyes on her.

'That's part of it.' She gathered her thoughts. 'From the start I knew where I stood with you. You never try to hide things I might dislike, or dress things up in fancy words.' She paused, realising she still hadn't got to the nub of it. 'You respect me. That first day on the beach you realised I might feel threatened and you deliberately set out to ease my fears and put limits on your behaviour. Some men wouldn't have done that.'

Some men would have tried to force her into acquiescence.

'It's a small enough thing. I don't like people who say one thing in public and do another in private.' His voice sounded grim, as if she'd touched a nerve.

'Exactly. There are too many who lie to get what they want. I admire that you don't, Strato.'

Even if increasingly she wanted more than he offered.

She yearned to understand him. Would he one day trust her enough to share his feelings and his past?

'Thank you, *Coritsa*.' He unfolded his arms. In the darkness his gaze held hers. 'Are you going to tell me about the person you're comparing me to?'

'How do you know there was someone—?'

'You speak so passionately. From experience. Someone hurt you.'

She'd never spoken about it, never wanted to. But suddenly she wanted to share. To feel less alone. Maybe that would complete the healing Strato had unwittingly begun. Perhaps it might encourage him to share too.

'His name was Adrian and I worked on his father's yacht in the Caribbean between research positions.'

'Let me guess.' Strato's voice hardened. 'He seduced you.'

Cora nodded. 'He was handsome, rich and privileged, used to getting whatever he wanted. You reminded me of him that first day.'

'I suspect that's not a compliment.'

She shrugged. 'He was also attentive, polite and friendly. I was wary, though. We came from separate worlds and I refused to fall for his charm.'

'Which increased his determination to have you.'

'I didn't realise it at first. I thought his persistence and patience meant he cared. I was naïve.'

'What happened?' Cora couldn't pinpoint the change in Strato's tone except she wondered if he spoke through gritted teeth.

'We had an affair. I thought it was more. I was falling for him and thought he felt the same.' She felt anger and something like shame at being so gullible. 'It wasn't till his friend came on board that I realised that for him I was just a convenient body. A notch on his bedpost.'

A shudder scraped her spine as she remembered overhearing Adrian talking to Brad about her. Not as his girlfriend but in the crudest terms about her body. Comparing her to other women he'd had. She'd felt like an animal at market, appraised by potential buyers.

'He offered me to his friend as if I were...'

A large hand covered hers, squeezing hard. 'I get the picture.'

Cora's heart hammered but she was determined to finish. She should have told someone long ago. She didn't want sympathy, but finally sharing this would ease the hurt she'd felt so long.

'When I refused, Adrian was annoyed, as if I'd insulted him or let him down. Later, after he'd given the rest of the crew the night off to go ashore, he came to me full of apologies, saying he hadn't meant to insult me. He said he knew I'd like Brad once I knew him better and suggested a threesome *to break the ice*!' She almost gagged on the words. 'He wasn't happy when I refused.'

'Did he hurt you?' No mistaking Strato's tone now. He was furious, yet his hands grasping both of hers were gentle. 'Tell me his name and I'll deal with him.'

'No need.' Though remembering Adrian's ugly look and his friend Brad's excited leer, she knew she'd been lucky to get away. Adrian wasn't used to being denied and the pair had cornered her. 'One of the crew was still aboard, heard the argument and came to help me. I left straight away.'

'You were all right?'

'I was fine.' She'd been shaken and sick with disgust but okay. Strange that *she'd* been the one to feel shamed by what had happened.

'It's a wonder you even spoke to me that first day. If you thought me like him.' Strato's voice was tight.

Cora shook her head. 'My brain was trying to warn me but the truth was…'

'Yes?' He leaned nearer.

'I was fascinated.' She'd never known such a profound or instantaneous reaction to any man. 'Logic told me to be careful but there was something about you I couldn't resist.'

Strato threaded his fingers through hers. 'That's how I felt. Fascinated. Even after you sent me packing I spent weeks thinking about you.' His voice dropped to a low note that scoured her soul. 'I couldn't get you out of my head. It was a new experience.'

Her breathing shallowed. She wanted to ask if it still felt unique to him. Because her feelings for Strato were unprecedented. She knew with a certainty she couldn't explain that for her this was serious.

'Ah, here we are.'

Disappointment mingled with relief filtered through her. No time now to ask about his feelings, but that meant he wouldn't disappoint her by saying his emotions weren't involved and for him this was still purely sexual.

It didn't feel as if it was simply lust between them as he ushered her aboard, his arm protectively around her. Nor when he led her by the hand to his bed and stood, staring down at her with gleaming eyes, as if seeing right into her heart.

Lust was there in the faint tremor of his hands as he unzipped her and in the harsh angle of his jaw. But so was tenderness and respect as he brushed his lips slowly across her bare shoulders, taking his time to caress her till she shivered with eagerness. In the way he slowly skimmed the crimson satin off her body then stood with something like wonder in his eyes as he took her in. As if she weren't an ordinary woman but some goddess who'd struck him dumb.

There was delicacy in the way he knelt to undo her sandals, and in the skimming, tantalising, delicious kisses he imprinted on her calves, knees and thighs.

There was even something like reverence in Strato's sigh as he hooked his thumbs into her thong and slid it down her trembling body.

And when he scooped her up in his arms, his eyes holding hers, Cora felt her heart swell against her ribs as if her bones had shrunk, or the feelings she harboured grew too big to hold in.

Soon she was naked on the bed and Strato made short work of his dinner suit. Even shorter work of protection. Still he didn't rush, but prowled up her body, nuzzling, kissing, stroking, till she was gasping for breath and pleading.

Strato wouldn't be hurried. But this wasn't like other times when she'd seen a teasing gleam in his eyes. Now his expression was intent, each caress considered and careful.

Was it crazy to think he was *showing* her his feelings though no words passed his lips? That those feelings were deeper than light-hearted flirtation?

When, finally, he settled between her thighs, propped on his elbows so she didn't take his full weight, his expression was grave. Cora saw furrows on his forehead and deep grooves bracket his gorgeous mouth and felt a moment of unspoken communion when she could swear their pulses beat as one.

Then his mouth broke into a slow smile that undid the last, fragile thread of her defences.

Cora smiled back.

Nothing in her life had been as good as this, here, now, with Strato. He undid her. Yet, as their bodies merged in one slow, sure stroke, she didn't feel undone but complete and stronger than she'd ever been in her life.

Together they made a whole that surpassed everything.

Cora planted a hand on his thrumming heart and lifted her other hand to his cheek, losing her breath as he turned his face into her touch and kissed her palm.

Tenderness welled along with anticipation.

She'd fallen for Strato. So deeply, so completely it put what she'd felt for Adrian in stark perspective. He'd flattered and tempted her, playing on her natural curiosity and burgeoning sexuality. But he'd only hurt her pride, not anything more significant.

Strato's fluid, powerful movements had her clinging, lifting her body into his rhythm and holding tight, eager not just for bliss but also for these moments of profound connection that felt as if they changed her for ever.

Did they change him too?

No time to think about it as he gathered her closer, his body leading hers deeper into pleasure, his eyes holding a promise she couldn't look away from.

'Coritsa.' His voice, velvet-wrapped gravel, was a caress in itself. The heated glow of his gaze as it held hers felt portentous.

'Strato, I…'

Suddenly it was upon them. The lightning bolt that turned the world iridescent. The shimmering wave upon wave upon wave of completion so exquisite it stole her voice. And still Strato held her eyes. Till finally, on one last explosive shudder, Cora tumbled into darkness.

As she sank into oblivion the words she hadn't said aloud echoed in her head.

Strato, I love you.

Her world had changed for ever.

CHAPTER TWELVE

DAYS LATER THEY were on the island of Aegina and Cora couldn't stop smiling.

Since leaving Athens things between her and Strato felt different. He was as attentive and passionate, as charming and as much fun. But there was an unspoken undercurrent that fed her excitement.

She didn't try to label it, for it had been scary enough, naming her feelings for him. She didn't want to con herself into believing he felt more than he did, or build too much upon his various kindnesses. Or the fact he'd asked her to stay past the agreed month.

It had been that night when they'd left Athens. Cora was sprawled, boneless, across Strato's big frame, his heart beating beneath her ear, when he'd asked her to stay. Not for a set time, but simply to stay.

Eagerness had vied with practicalities, like worries over her stalled career and the need to see her father, but her biggest concern was of digging herself deeper into an emotional hole.

What if Strato never returned her feelings?

Yet Cora hadn't been able to say no. She knew this man, enigmatic as he could be, was the man for her.

Add to that her father was well and had help at the

hotel. Strato had also promised to sail back so she could check on her father in person instead of via her regular calls.

As for her career as a marine biologist, that was harder. She'd left work to help her father and there weren't many other positions around. She should be looking but for now she couldn't think past the present and Strato.

It was a shock to realise they'd been together just over a month.

A month during which she'd had no period.

They stood before the beautiful Temple of Aphaia, high on a hill overlooking the Aegean Sea, the scent of pines and sea salt wafting on the breeze. Strato was beside her, strong and solid. Just as well, for she rocked back on her heels as realisation hit.

Frantically she recalculated the weeks, flicking through dates in her head, and with each recalculation shock edged further along her bones, like the shadow of a cloud creeping across the sun.

Her periods were clockwork-regular.

Which meant...

'Cora, are you okay?'

Sea-green eyes met hers and a warm hand gripped her arm. The concern she saw in Strato's expression calmed her.

'Yes, absolutely fine.'

There was no need to panic.

This had been the most amazing, unusual month of her life. Would it be so surprising if her body didn't follow its usual rhythms? She didn't feel different physically.

And even if there *was* a reason for her delayed period, she and Strato weren't passing strangers. They'd moved on from their original insta-lust. Pregnancy might even be the impetus for acknowledging a deeper relationship.

Yet, thinking the word *pregnancy* sent a quiver of shock through her.

She'd assumed that when she had a child she'd be in a secure relationship like her parents had shared.

But she was getting ahead of herself. First she had to find out if there was a child.

Would the small town where they'd come ashore sell pregnancy test kits? Cora took a slow breath, trying to calm her racing thoughts. She'd have to get to a bigger town and find out if she was pregnant.

Then, well, she'd think about what came next if it happened.

Strato stood on his private deck, a cold beer in one hand. Where was Cora? Usually she'd joined him on deck by now. The sun was low in the sky.

He felt restless because, after their early morning sightseeing trip to the temple, he'd devoted himself to work while Cora took a hired car to the other side of the island. Usually they explored together. This was the first time they'd been separated for any length of time, apart from that afternoon in Athens.

Strange to think he'd become so accustomed to her company that he noticed an absence of a few hours. He sometimes worked alone in his study and that didn't bother him.

Because always she'd been nearby. Accessible.

His glass stopped halfway to his mouth then lowered.

Suddenly the taste in his mouth wasn't the tang of beer but something bitter and dank.

He wasn't becoming obsessive about her, was he? Needing to know where she was every moment? Needing to control her movements?

His belly clenched as if in response to an invisible blow. His stomach curdled.

Strato waited for logic to reassure him. Obsession was impossible. It had to be. Because he, of all people, knew how dangerous it was. His skin prickled and searing pain shot through his shoulder, even though the scar tissue there was old.

Again he swallowed.

Could such a fatal flaw run in families? He'd told himself it couldn't, not if you did everything you could to guard against it. And Strato had done everything to prevent that happening.

Still he frowned. It was true his relationship with Cora had altered. She was no longer a casual sexual partner.

As if! From the first he'd felt anything but casual about her.

But he'd been sure that though she'd become a friend as much as a lover, she only occupied a specific part in his life. Strato had honed the ability to compartmentalise his world.

Yet today he'd found himself wondering what she was doing. Whether he wouldn't rather be with her. Regretting their time apart.

Movement caught his eye. It was Cora, emerging on deck. He turned fully and was instantly swamped by his response to her.

Good old sexual desire. Admiration. Joy.

Surely they were all positives? Surely that negated the secret fear that his feelings verged on something dark?

'You look fabulous.' His voice was gruff with appreciation. Instead of her usual casual clothes she wore a bronze-coloured dress, gleaming like silk. Its narrow straps left her shoulders bare and its cut followed her body, cinching in around her narrow waist before spilling gracefully over her hips and thighs.

Beyond her stretched the green-blue sea and above it, at the top of the hill overlooking the coast, the white marble columns of the ruined temple.

The setting suited her. He'd first imagined her as a sea nymph, so much more than an ordinary mortal woman. Seeing her against that backdrop reinforced that feeling.

Cora was special.

Want rose in him, the familiar tide of desire, but something extra too. Something warm and tender.

Strato refused to analyse it. Instead he put his glass down and approached her, taking her hands in his. 'I approve. You bought it today?'

She shook her head and for the first time in weeks he couldn't read her expression. 'I got it in Athens.'

She'd spent his money well.

'And you waited till now to wear it?' He bent his head and kissed her, slowly and thoroughly, only drawing back when he realised he was on the verge of sweeping her into his arms and straight to bed.

He was determined to prove he could control his feelings around Cora.

She shrugged and he realised that, despite the way she'd melted into his kiss, the movement looked stiff.

'Have you spoken to your father today? Is all okay at the hotel?'

'Yes and yes. Both are thriving. Thank you, Strato.' Her expression eased. Maybe he'd imagined tension because he'd been distracted by his own troubling thoughts.

'Good. Now, what would you like to drink?'

'Sparkling water, thanks.'

He nodded and made himself release her, knowing that he'd much prefer to keep touching her. Again that tiny quiver of concern flickered through him.

Strange that the silence as he went to the bar and got her drink felt heavy. Usually he and Cora chatted easily but didn't feel the need to fill every moment with talk. He turned, her glass in his hand, and saw he hadn't imagined it. Something was wrong. Cora bit the corner of her mouth and her shoulders were hunched.

'What is it, *Coritsa*? Is something wrong?' He couldn't imagine what. Things were good between them.

Yet to his dismay she nodded. 'Not wrong exactly but…' She drew a deep breath that made her breasts rise high. 'We need to talk. Maybe we should sit down.'

Perhaps it was his unresolved tension from earlier, or a sixth sense for trouble, but Strato felt his own shoulders tighten. 'Don't prevaricate. Just tell me.'

She swallowed and finally nodded, her eyes not leaving his. 'I'm pregnant.'

There was a crashing sound but Strato didn't really register it. He was too busy watching the woman before him looking so earnest as her words, her unbelievable words, echoed in his brain.

Something inside him plummeted.

Had he really thought she was different?

Had he really believed in the happiness he'd found with her?

She'd prepared carefully for this moment, he realised, looking again at that slinky, seductive dress that was so different from her usual outfits. It turned her into a different woman. More like the others who'd tried over the years to catch him.

Had the woman who'd snared his interest on that tiny island, the fascinating, forthright woman who cared more about protecting sea turtle nesting sites than about jewels and his vast fortune, been an illusion? Had their chance meeting and her initial rejection been part of a deliberate ploy, to attract then hook him?

Pain stabbed his chest as his lungs failed.

How many times had a woman stood before him, claiming to carry his child?

Strato shut his eyes because even now the sight of Cora, gorgeous and tempting, messed with his head. As if what she said could be possible.

That only made things worse because the idea of him fathering a child was the stuff of nightmares. Clammy heat crept across his skin and nausea welled.

He snapped his eyes open.

At least he was spared that horror. He'd made sure there'd be no children. He was the last of his family.

But that meant Cora was lying. Like those others who'd tried to snare him in marriage.

He hauled in a rough breath.

He didn't want to believe it. *Not Cora.*

But Strato knew about betrayal. He knew it so well it was inked onto his very bones, etched on his skin.

He understood you could rely on no one but yourself.

How had he forgotten the lesson that shaped his life?

Yet watching Cora, as all the good things he'd experienced with her crumbled into dust, felt like a blow from which he'd never recover.

Because he'd let her get under his skin. Let himself be tempted into feeling too much.

It was his fault as much as hers.

Cora watched the glass drop to the deck and shatter but Strato didn't seem to notice.

The concern in his eyes died, replaced by the shock she'd expected and something else. It looked like pain.

She frowned, heart hammering, trying to gauge his response. It couldn't be pain. That made no sense.

Then he shut his eyes, breathing deep, nostrils flaring and hands curling at his sides. He looked like a man struggling with strong emotion.

Cora wanted to go to him, touch him, *connect* with him. But she stood rooted to the spot. Something about the starkness of his features and the lines ploughing his forehead held her back.

Then he was staring at her again, eyes narrowed and hard as chips of stone.

Not a delighted father-to-be, then.

'You're the third.' His voice was barely recognisable. Raw and rough and once more she sensed pain. Yet his eyes were frigid with accusation.

'Third what?'

His mouth stretched wide in a humourless smile that made her heart twist.

'Third woman to tell me she's having my child.'

'You've already got children?' Her hand went to her throat in shock. It was only when his gaze lowered that she realised her other hand had gone instinctively to her stomach, as if comforting the new life deep inside.

Even now, hours after confirming her pregnancy, Cora reeled from the revelation. It didn't seem real. Her body felt the same as ever.

Yet, in the short space of time since she'd learned about the baby, it seemed she'd acquired protective, maternal instincts. Instincts that urged her to retreat from this big man.

Except she knew Strato. Knew he'd never hurt her or their baby.

Nevertheless, his tight smile perturbed her. She'd never seen him like this.

'No, I don't have kids. I told you, I'll never have a family.'

Cora waited for an explanation but none came. Had the babies died? Horror filled her. 'What happened?'

'Nothing. The women left when I wouldn't marry them.'

She shook her head. 'The babies! What happened to the babies?' She felt as if she were underwater, sounds blurred and distant, struggling to make herself understood.

'There were no babies.' He flicked a glance at her abdomen once more then back to her face. 'One woman wasn't even pregnant. The other was, but to someone else.' His lips drew back in something like a snarl. 'They made a mistake thinking they could lie their way into a share of my fortune.'

Shock slammed into her. 'You think I'm lying? You think I invented this?'

After what they'd shared, not only their bodies but

the growing emotional intimacy, Cora felt sick at his implication.

'I *know* you're lying.' Before she could protest he went on, his expression grim. 'I should have known. Believe it or not, I thought you different.' He shook his head and she almost believed she saw sorrow on his face.

'Listen, Strato, I know this is a shock. I was stunned too when I found out today.' Cora told herself it wasn't surprising a man who'd faced false paternity claims should react badly, though something within her shrank at his forbidding expression.

'You only found out today?' He shoved his hands into his trouser pockets. 'How convenient that you happened to have a sexy new dress to wear while you announced the news.' His tone dripped sarcasm. 'What did you expect? That I'd be so overcome by lust that I wouldn't care you're lying? That I didn't mean it when I said I'd never have a family?'

The shivers rippling across her flesh became shudders and she folded her arms, partly for warmth and partly in anger at his hurtful accusations.

'I don't know what I expected. But it wasn't this... viciousness.'

Strato folded his arms too. On him the gesture didn't look defensive but aggressive, showcasing the formidable strength in his arms and upper body. 'Lady, you have no idea if you think *this* is vicious. Be thankful you don't.'

Her chin hiked higher. 'I have no wish to see it. This is bad enough.' She swallowed hard. 'I understand you've had bad experiences but I'm not lying, Strato. When have I ever lied to you?'

For a moment she wondered if she might have got through to him. Until he spoke.

'That's one of the things I admired about you, Cora. That you were honest. Or appeared to be. But I *know* this is a lie because I can't have children.'

'Sorry?'

'I had a vasectomy. I'll never have children.'

Cora stared, trying to take this in. Her sense of unreality, which had begun with the news of the pregnancy, then crested when Strato turned into a man she didn't know, battered at her.

'But I'm pregnant. The baby is yours.' He said nothing, merely lifted one eyebrow haughtily. 'You used condoms against pregnancy.'

'No, I used them because I've had multiple partners. It's a common-sense health precaution.'

Cora reeled. That put her in her place. One of his multiple partners. Her skin crawled. She'd actually begun to believe they shared something special!

Then the implications sank in. He'd had a vasectomy and used condoms and *still* she'd got pregnant? What were the chances?

For a second she was tempted to think maybe he was right and there was a mistake. Except she'd bought two test kits, two different brands, and each time got the same result. Plus there was that time weeks ago when the condom broke.

'That's silenced you, hasn't it?' Strato's voice was flinty, yet she imagined she heard something more than anger there. She peered up into his eyes, but could see no softening.

It was like looking into the face of a stranger, a stern, disapproving stranger.

Incredible how much that hurt. So much that she felt it as a searing physical pain right through her middle. The change in him, from caring, fun, attentive lover to brooding enemy was too much to take in.

'No, Strato, it hasn't silenced me, because I'm telling the truth.' She gulped a deep breath and focused on keeping her voice even. 'I bought a couple of pregnancy kits today and took multiple tests to be sure. Because, believe it or not, pregnancy wasn't in my plans. At least not yet. I can show you the results.'

Still he said nothing, just looked down that straight nose at her as if he were a judge and she a criminal.

She'd been right to be nervous about breaking the news. So nervous she'd taken refuge in fancy clothes, hoping to boost her confidence. From his expression it wouldn't matter what she said, Strato wouldn't believe her.

She was torn between outrage and sorrow. It was obvious she'd deluded herself, thinking he might return her feelings.

'I haven't been with a man in years.' Not since Adrian, who'd hurt her so badly. 'Until you.'

Her eyes flickered shut for a second. The pain Adrian had inflicted was nothing to the damage Strato was doing now.

Oh, she could sure pick men! Her lips pulled back in a grimace. First Adrian and now another arrogant rich man, who, it seemed, didn't care for her either.

Why, oh, why hadn't she followed her instinct and refused Strato?

Because from the start he fascinated you. Because with him you felt like a stronger, better, happier ver-

sion of yourself. Not the cautious, hemmed-in person
you became after Adrian.

Much good that had done her!

'It's no good, Cora. Whatever so-called proof you
have, I know it will be manufactured. It won't stand
up to scrutiny.'

'But you can't brush it off like that! Not after what
we've shared. This is a *baby*, not a con! You're going
to be a father.'

She'd hoped to crack that icy control and she suc-
ceeded. But not in the way she hoped. Strato didn't
soften. He didn't offer to submit to a paternity test. Instead that cold stare turned to flashing fire and a look
that scorched her to the soles of her feet.

'If you think to appeal to my emotions, you've mis-
stepped, Cora. I can't think of anything that horrifies
me more than the idea of fathering a child.'

Her throat constricted, making it difficult to swallow.
There was no trace now of the charismatic man she'd
fallen in love with. No tenderness. Only harsh, horrible
words and a terrible blankness in his eyes.

'Now get out of my sight. I'll arrange for you to leave
in the morning.'

CHAPTER THIRTEEN

CORA DIDN'T WAIT till the morning. Strato emerged next day, red-eyed from too much brandy and lack of sleep, to be told she'd gone ashore the previous night.

Something grabbed at his vitals, twisting till pain screamed through him.

He told himself he was angry she'd run off in the night. Yet beneath the multiple layers of fury at her for lying, at himself for falling for those lies, and anguish at the terrible memories she'd stirred, was fear.

Fear that something bad might happen to her.

Logic said that she'd easily find accommodation in the little coastal town. Of course she was safe. This wasn't a dangerous area and she was a capable woman. She was probably already crossing the island to catch the Athens ferry.

Yet anxiety lingered. She was alone and upset.

As if her story were true! Strato reminded himself Cora had spun a deceitful tale. Yet she'd been almost convincing with that stark look of dismay and dawning hurt.

He'd almost fallen for her game. Though clearly her story was impossible.

Strato hated being played for a sucker, especially as,

for the first time he could recall, he'd come to like having a woman around. Cora wasn't precisely restful, but with her he felt…

He ground his teeth at the way his thoughts kept straying to the good times they'd had. How could that be when those were obviously manufactured like her tale about a child?

That was what really undid him. He'd been lied to so often by scheming women, but for a second when she broke her news he'd actually imagined it might be real. Imagined he might be on the brink of fatherhood.

Him, a father. Carrying the legacy of his father before him.

Horror hurled him back in time to the atrocity he'd made it his life's work to forget.

You'll never forget, Doukas. The best you can do is pretend it never happened.

It had worked for twenty-five years.

Yet the one time he'd shut his eyes last night, nightmares of the past had taken him straight back to hell.

He spun around. He needed another drink. Something to deaden the hurt Cora had caused and stop the traumatic memories she'd unleashed.

Except how could he hide with the memory of Cora standing before him with those earnest, soulful eyes, telling him they were going to have a child?

Even so, he called Manoli to him and told him to go ashore and check that Cora had spent the night at one of the local hotels.

'And if she didn't?' His assistant's expression was stiff, a reminder that he, too, had liked Cora. From his withering stare Strato knew he blamed his boss for her sudden disappearance.

The downside of having an employee who was so close, as close as Strato got to a friend, was that he wasn't afraid to share his opinions.

Now he thought about it, all the staff had liked her.

'Then use your initiative, damn it! I need to know she's safely on her way home.' Even if he had no intention of seeing her again.

Slowly Manoli nodded. 'And shall I give her a message if I find her…sir?'

The fake obsequiousness of that *sir* was a deliberate provocation from a man who'd used his first name for years.

'Don't push it, Manoli.' Strato growled and headed for the bar. 'I had my reasons for sending her away.'

Excellent reasons.

Yet that didn't make him feel better. Even when Manoli reported that Cora had spent the night in a budget hotel then caught the first bus to the other side of the island to catch the Athens ferry, Strato couldn't settle.

So, on the spur of the moment they sailed to Alexandria. Though once there Strato found he didn't feel in the mood for Egypt's attractions. Instead they went to Monte Carlo. It was only when they arrived that he recalled he was bored with the place. Spain was next but Strato couldn't find the distraction he sought.

Work didn't fulfil him. He found himself constantly distracted, even in high-level negotiations, till he forced himself to step back and delegate more, rather than undo the good work of others with rash decisions.

He was on the point of flying to Rarotonga, simply for a change of scenery, when he realised what he was doing.

Running away.

Looking for something to fill the void in his life left by Cora. Not that he was searching for another woman. Hell, no! But the ennui that had dogged him before he met her was back full force. The listless sense of pointlessness. Nothing, not even business, interested him. He couldn't settle to anything.

Because even now you can't quite believe she's like the rest, can you, Doukas?

He gritted his teeth and took a long swallow of iced water, having decided to stop drinking alcohol when that did nothing to ease his mind or his mood.

Music reached him across the marina. Someone was having a party on one of the nearby superyachts. But the sound of laughter didn't entice him.

He frowned into the twilight, trying to remember which port this was. There'd been so many in the last few weeks.

It didn't matter. What mattered was that niggling sense of something left undone.

Strato prided himself on following his instincts. When he got the feeling something wasn't right about a deal he delved deeper and always discovered a sound reason for that warning burr across his nape.

He felt it now but it had nothing to do with the company. It had to do with Cora.

He didn't understand it. It was impossible that he'd got her pregnant. There was no way, no way at all. Not after a vasectomy and then condoms…the idea was laughable.

Yet that sixth sense bristled the hairs across his nape and all the way down his arms.

Finally Strato grabbed his phone. It took a while to get the person he wanted. It was out of business hours but his name made most things possible. Finally he put his question.

It was as he'd thought. Impossible that he'd impregnated Cora.

Well, the doctor amended, *almost* impossible. There were occasional, rare cases...

Strato's mind blanked, the voice at the other end of the line blurring.

The music from across the marina became a buzz of white noise. The lights dimmed. There was a sound in Strato's ears, a hammering that grew faster and louder, till he realised he'd forgotten to breathe and dragged a desperate breath into aching lungs. Immediately the thump of his pulse eased enough for him to hear the medico's words.

'So you're saying...' Strato found his voice '...that it's extremely unlikely but you can't rule out the possibility.'

'Exactly.'

Strato braced himself against the deck's railing with a trembling hand as regret washed through him. Regret at how he'd treated Cora.

And fear. Fear that the one thing he'd been determined to avoid might actually come to pass.

Cora was helping Doris tidy the kitchen after evening service when one of the part-time waitresses came in from the now-empty restaurant.

'There's someone to see you, Cora.' Her breathless voice made Cora look up from the plates she was stacking.

'Who is it?' Clearly someone interesting, given the gleam in her dark eyes.

'A man. And what a man.' She shook her hand as if it burned. 'A tall, handsome stranger. And that sexy voice!' She gave a little shiver.

Cora barely noticed because she was too busy staring at the empty doorway behind the woman, heart in mouth as she imagined who could have caused such a reaction.

The answer was obvious. Strato.

But that was impossible. He'd washed his hands of her. He'd all but tossed her off his yacht, ordering her out of his sight.

The memory stirred indignation as well as hurt. Cora's shoulders tightened and her hands clenched. He might be rich but he had no right to treat her that way.

For the first time in her pregnancy she felt nauseous.

Could it be Strato? Who else could cause such a stir?

'Well…' Doris watched her from shrewd eyes '…aren't you going to go and see who it is?'

Cora was tempted to say no, she wasn't.

She didn't want to talk to Strato ever again.

Who are you kidding? You might be fuming with anger, but you've got unfinished business with him. Despite everything, you want to see him, don't you?

Actually, she wanted to punch him and rant at him for what he'd done but part of her actually missed him. It had been almost impossible to settle in the weeks since she'd left him. She'd been so distracted she knew that only the fact the hotel was frantically busy had saved her from her father noticing. But Doris clearly sensed something was wrong.

'Of course. Are you okay to finish up?' She untied her apron and tossed it into the laundry basket.

'Sure. We're almost done. Don't you want to tidy your hair?'

She did. She'd like to face this man looking poised and elegant, but she refused to let him think she'd put in a special effort for his sake. So she shook her head, wished the others goodnight and marched out of the kitchen and into the restaurant. It was empty so she went out onto the terrace.

Most of the lights were off, leaving the illumination from a single rope of fairy lights strung along the edge of the vine-laden trellis. In the distance the lights of the village spilled across the bay's still waters and out at the point she picked out a large vessel.

'Hello, Cora.'

It was him!

She swallowed, hating the way her throat constricted with emotion.

Cora turned and there he was, tall and still, hands thrust in his trouser pockets. Her gaze tracked his wide shoulders and firm chin. His mouth set hard and tight, the frown furrowing his brow.

If she'd had any thought that he was happy to be here she could forget it. He looked anything but.

Cora folded her arms. 'Why are you here?' Her tone was sharp. Good, she didn't want him realising how conflicted she felt.

'To talk. To apologise.'

Her heart skipped a beat, yet nothing in his voice indicated he wanted to be here. So much for her fantasy of him begging her forgiveness because he realised how much she meant to him.

She drew herself up sharply. 'Not here.' With the hotel full, they could be overheard by anyone in the floors above. Not looking at him, she strode across the terrace, out past the tamarisks towards the water.

Strato fell into step beside her as she followed the path away from the harbour, towards the deserted promontory, bright moonlight illuminating the way. Cora tried not to notice how familiar it felt, walking beside him, his tantalising scent teasing her.

'You left your visit very late. I'm about to go to bed.' Instantly she regretted the words, thinking of all those evenings that had ended with them together in bed, lost to everything but the delight they'd shared. How she'd felt cherished.

Until he'd brutally rejected her, calling her a liar and worse.

'I just arrived and came straight to see you.'

'If you expect me to be impressed, I'm not.' She drew a breath, trying to slow her racing heartbeat. 'Just say what you came to say.'

Silence followed her words.

Had he expected a warmer welcome?

Her mouth twisted as she thought of her anguish because the man she'd fallen in love with despised her. He hadn't even considered the possibility she told the truth.

'I'm sorry, Cora. I shouldn't have ordered you off the yacht like that.'

To her amazement, Strato sounded as if he really meant it. As if, like she, he was stressed and worried.

Her step faltered and she forced herself to look at the sea rather than at him. They'd stopped near a stand of dark trees that hid them from the hotel. All was silent except for the soft shush of the water and, floating across the bay, the faint sound of music.

'Really? You left it a long time to apologise.'

The first week she'd been on tenterhooks, hoping he'd contact her. But he'd meant every cutting word about her lying and trying to snare him.

As if anyone could snare this man who didn't trust!

'I was utterly convinced I couldn't father a child.'

'What changed?'

In her peripheral vision she saw him raise his arm to rub the back of his neck. 'I got medical advice. It's rare but occasionally a vasectomy isn't successful.'

He paused and she said nothing. After all, she already knew he'd fathered her child. She'd had weeks to convince herself it was as well he wanted nothing to do with her baby. She'd bring it up herself, here on her island, where it would be loved and cared for.

'And?'

'And I had a check-up. It turns out that mine is one of those rare cases.' His tone was so sombre it raised the hair on her arms and across her neck. 'There's an outside chance I could father a child.'

Cora felt like shouting it wasn't a chance. It was a reality. One she lived with every day, as she fought to acclimatise to the fact she was pregnant. Early next year she'd be a mother.

She'd alternated between fear and excitement. She knew nothing about babies and this was going to affect her plans to return to marine biology. But her father and Doris would stand by her when she told them. Her child would have a stable, loving home, even without its father on the scene.

'You don't say anything.'

She swung around. 'What do you want me to say, Strato? You're not telling me anything I don't know. *I'm* the one whose whole life has changed because I'm carrying *your* child.' Her index finger drilled hard against his breastbone.

Before she could pull back he covered her hand with his. Cora was shocked at how warm and familiar it felt. Shocked at how something in her eased at his touch. How much she wanted from him, even now.

The realisation made her yank her hand free and step back. This man destroyed her in so many ways.

Pain engulfed her. She'd fallen for Strato, believing him to be something he wasn't. Which confirmed her appalling taste in men. Twice she'd made a terrible mistake, gulled into believing someone selfish and over-privileged might care about her.

She tilted her chin to meet his stare. 'You've said you're sorry. Now what?' His apology didn't change anything fundamental. 'I notice you admit you *could* be the father, not that you are.'

Strato lifted his shoulders. 'There's a big difference between the two.'

Cora's hands jammed on her hips. 'You really are some piece of work, Strato. You come all this way and admit you overreacted but still you don't believe me.' She dragged in a rough breath, made difficult by the way her lungs cramped, pain shooting behind her ribs. 'It's as if you *want* to believe I'm lying.'

To her surprise, he shifted, his gaze leaving hers.

She was right! He'd prefer to believe she was a gold-digger. The realisation loosened her knees and she had to concentrate on staying upright.

'The one thing in this world that I want to avoid is becoming a father.' His deep voice was rough with what sounded like genuine emotion.

Why was that so important to him? She'd pondered that from every angle and had no answer.

'What are you after? A paternity test? You're trying to prove, even now, that the baby isn't yours?'

As soon as she said it she realised she'd hit the nail on the head. It was there in his stillness, that searching scrutiny so intense that she felt it even in the silver wash of moonlight.

'Is it so unreasonable?' He spread his hands palm up. 'The odds are against it, since I used a condom every time. And I've already had two women claim to be pregnant with my child.'

But I'm not like them!

Cora wanted to shriek the words, barely managing to hold them back.

'I see.' It took everything she had to keep her hands on her hips rather than wrapping her arms defensively around herself.

He cared so little for her that he *wanted* her to be a liar, so he could walk back to his hedonistic life without a backward glance. Her baby deserved better than this man as its father.

'And if I refuse?'

'Why would you refuse the chance to prove I'm the father? There's no risk to the child. All it takes is a blood test from you. And if I am the father...' he paused and she watched him breathe deep as if collecting himself '...then I'll provide support.'

'Money, you mean.' Because clearly he wouldn't be a real father, bonding with their baby and being there through thick and thin.

The fight went out of her. Cora's shoulders slumped

as exhaustion hit. She'd known they had no future, yet she'd hoped. Now she saw how futile those hopes were.

She shook her head, about to turn away, then stopped.

Was that the responsible thing to do? She remembered how close they'd come to losing the family business, how tenuous her scientific career would be once she took more time off to have a child. What if there was another downturn and they lost the hotel? Sometime in the future her child might need financial help from its father.

So she made herself ask about the paternity test.

Unsurprisingly Strato had someone on his yacht who could visit the next day to take a blood sample then return to Athens to have the results processed.

For what felt like a full minute she hesitated, fighting outrage. Finally she nodded. 'I'll do it. But just send the doctor. I don't want to see you.'

She'd prove this baby was Strato's in case their child ever needed his support, but then she'd cut him from her life. He didn't want her and didn't want to be a father. Well, that was fine with her.

It *had* to be fine. For she had no choice in the matter.

Cora spun on her heel and marched, alone, along the well-trodden path home. She ignored the wetness trailing down her cheeks and the terrible pain inside as if her heart had cracked in two.

CHAPTER FOURTEEN

DAYS LATER CORA took a couple of hours off for an early morning trip to her favourite islet. It was probably too early to see turtle hatchlings, but she needed time alone.

Since seeing Strato she found it impossible to settle. Even when she was busy working at the hotel her thoughts strayed to him. To his apology that was only half an apology, for he still didn't trust her. To the feeling she'd had that something was badly wrong, the tension in his tall frame evident even in the moonlight.

Wrong? Of course there was something wrong! He was convinced she was a gold-digger. It was crazy that she felt even a spark of concern for him. *She* was the injured party, and the one who'd bear the consequences.

Setting her jaw, she lifted her water bottle and drank, grateful for the shade of the trees at the edge of the tiny beach.

Surely in this peaceful spot she could think clearly about her future as a single mother. As yet she hadn't noticed any physical changes but soon they'd come. She needed to think about preparing for the baby. Until now her thoughts had been a jumble, as concerned with her failed relationship with Strato as with the baby.

'Hello, Cora.' The deep voice came from behind her. She spun around, spilling water, and gaped.

For this was Strato as she'd never seen him. Still tall and handsome in his casual clothes, but his features were etched with lines that carved deep around his mouth and furrowed his brow. He looked sombre. More than that. He looked like a man on the brink of disaster.

'Strato!' Her voice cracked. 'What is it?' She made to get up but he gestured for her to stay where she was, seating himself nearby.

'I've had the test results.' His voice was different, no longer smooth but scratchy and tense. 'I'm sorry. You didn't deserve my anger that night when all you did was tell the truth. I treated you very badly.'

'You did.'

'I apologise unreservedly.' His mouth hitched up at the corner in a smile that held no amusement. 'You needed support, not anger.'

Slowly she nodded. Yet it wasn't the way he'd treated her then that concerned her as much as his intentions now.

Cora knew they could never be a couple, no matter the hopes she'd held, or the fact that even now she saw him and wanted to smooth away that scowl and have him hold her as if he'd never let her go. But surely, sharing a child, they could build some trust, some level of friendship?

Stoically she ignored a piercing ache at the thought that was all they'd ever be. Strato had made his feelings, or lack of them, clear.

'I don't lie, Strato. I was always straight with you.'

'I know.' He shook his head. 'I tried so hard to believe you were like all the others, lying for personal gain. I even told myself the fact you accepted my money to buy those dresses was another proof against you.'

'But I—'

'It's okay, I know, Cora. I know now you didn't access my money, because you're too independent.' He shook his head and for a second she thought she read warmth in his expression. 'The fact was I simply didn't want to believe you.'

Cora put down the water bottle and clasped her hands. 'Because you don't want a child.'

He nodded but didn't offer anything more.

She waited, telling herself he'd eventually explain. There had to be a reason he'd turned from caring, considerate lover to fierce enemy in the blink of an eye.

'I'll support you,' he said finally, his shadowed gaze catching hers for a moment before moving on, looking down the beach in a way that made her think he didn't see it.

'What do you mean by support? Money?' *She* didn't want his money but wouldn't refuse the possibility of him helping their child when it was older. 'Moral support? Shared parenting?'

Cora couldn't miss his recoil at her last words. The way his jaw clenched so hard she saw the quick flick of his too-fast pulse.

'I'm not cut out to be a father. I told you that.' His eyes sought hers for a moment but instead of filling her with the usual warmth, that look left her chilled. 'But anything else I can provide. Money, security, a home—'

'I have a home. We'll live with my father and Doris, where I grew up.'

The idea should make her happy. Except for a brief

period she'd imagined a future with this man, this lover turned stranger.

'But what about your career? You can't get a marine biologist's job here.'

Cora frowned at his concern. How could the man who'd treated her so outrageously worry about such a thing? He confused her more than ever.

'I can't work elsewhere and keep the baby with me, so I've no choice.' Her smile was tight. 'It looks like my future will be in the hotel business.' It had been a dream to pursue her scientific work but some dreams just didn't come true.

'But I'll help financially. You can hire a full-time nanny. Live wherever you like—'

'No.' She breathed deep before continuing. 'I don't want your money, Strato. We'll do well enough.' She lifted her hand when he made to protest. 'I won't object to you providing support later, maybe for university. But I'll live on the island where I grew up. It's more important that our child has people who love it than a fancy house and a paid nanny.'

Strato's frown deepened at her words but he didn't object. Why should he? She was letting him off lightly.

'But there's one thing I do want.' Cora lifted her chin and fixed her gaze on his. 'I know you don't want to be a hands-on father.' Even though she sensed the man she'd fallen for, the caring, fun-loving man who'd ensured she had regular contact with her father and who'd worked so hard to seek out experiences she'd appreciate, would make a terrific dad. 'But I want our child to know you. To have a bond with you. I don't want our baby growing up only knowing you as a distant stranger in the news.'

Family was important. Cora cherished those years

when she'd had her mother. Though her relationship with her dad was special, she was grateful she'd had the chance to know and love both her parents. Strato might not be the man she'd hoped but she knew he had a caring side.

'All I ask is that you spend some time getting to know our child. Even just a couple of days now and then but on a regular basis.'

She resisted the urge to wrap her arms around herself, because what she was asking wasn't much for Strato but for her it would be torture, seeing him again and again, thinking of what might have been if he'd really been the man she hoped.

'I'm sorry, Cora. But I can't.'

'Can't?' Her temper flared. 'Surely you mean *won't*! Do you really care so little about the life we've created together, our *child*, that you can turn your back on it?'

'It's better that way.' His voice was harsh. 'Some people shouldn't be parents. Our baby will be better off without me.'

Cora heard it then. Pain. Strato's voice sounded scraped raw, as if it hurt to talk. If that weren't enough, the tension in his big frame spoke for itself.

'I don't believe that. Not of you, at any rate.' Strato was no Prince Charming, but he had lots of good qualities. So many she still, angry as she was, couldn't wash her hands of him.

He turned sharply, green eyes clashing with hers. For a second she thought she saw surprise there. Then his expression turned guarded and she couldn't read anything.

'It's true.' He paused. 'But I'll arrange for funds—'

'No!' Cora scrambled to her feet. 'I don't want your

money. I want the truth. You owe me that. Why don't you care enough to be a father to our child? I'm only asking for a couple of visits a year.'

She didn't know if she sounded furious or pleading. Maybe both.

Strato rose in a single lithe movement. 'You're going to keep prodding, aren't you?' His chest expanded mightily as if he struggled to contain his feelings.

'I'm simply asking you to explain. One day our child…' her throat tightened '…will want to know why you didn't care. I don't want them believing there's something wrong with them that made their father refuse to see them.'

His eyes widened as if he hadn't thought about that. But instead of answering, he took out his phone and typed something. Then, in silence, he scrolled, frowning, and scrolled some more.

'Here.' He handed it over.

Cora blinked at the screen then back at him, but he'd already turned away as if he didn't want to watch her read.

Man slays family!

The headline stopped her breath.

It was an old newspaper report from Brisbane about a murder-suicide. A man had been fighting his estranged wife for custody of their three children. There were accusations of violence and stalking against him. One night he got into the house where she was living, killed her, drugged their children and set fire to the house before killing himself. He'd intended them all to die together.

Cora shuddered at the appalling story, her flesh crawling. She'd heard of such violent acts but couldn't stifle a gasp of sheer horror. The only positive piece in the whole, dreadful tale was that one child had survived.

'I don't understand.' She lifted her eyes.

Strato stared straight back, his taut, beautiful face so grim her stomach curdled.

'I remember my grandfather, just. He made his wife's life hell. He died when I was young but he taught my father well.' Strato paused, and Cora realised he looked physically sick. 'That's my father in the article. The man who killed his family.'

'Your *father*?' She goggled up at him, as if she couldn't process his words. Strato couldn't blame her. It was such an obscene crime.

'Can you see the resemblance? I've got his looks, his height and strength.' Strato gritted his teeth, every word paining him. It was torture even to think of his father and grandfather, much less talk about them. 'There's a twisted streak in my family. I refuse to pass it on or hurt another generation.' He paused, letting that sink in. 'I don't dare risk being a father. It's too dangerous.'

Cora gaped. She looked down at the article then back at him. 'But this was in Australia and the family name isn't Doukas.'

Strato shrugged. 'My mother was Greek but we were born in Australia.' He paused, his mouth twisting. 'After *that*, I was adopted by my Greek aunt and uncle. I took their surname. I refused to use my father's name again.'

Changing his identity, putting the past behind him, had been the only way to survive. Even then, for years it had felt like a half-life. He'd wanted to connect with his aunt, who'd tried so hard with him, but something held him back.

The fear of getting close. The fear of caring too much. Of losing everything again.

Was it any wonder he was a loner? He socialised, he partied. There were even a few, a very few people he liked and trusted, like his faithful secretary Manoli and Damen Nicolaides, who could have been a competitor but instead was something like a friend. Or would be, if Strato trusted himself enough to have friendships.

Yet here was Cora, wanting him to be a *father*! As if that were possible.

The thought of it unwound something inside him that he couldn't allow. To the outside world Strato Doukas was the epitome of louche debauchery and self-indulgence. No one guessed at the soldered-shut lid he kept on his emotions. The fact that his inability to maintain permanent relationships was by choice, because he feared what they might reveal about him.

For his father's and grandfather's blood flowed in his veins.

That alone wouldn't make him dangerous. Upbringing accounted for a lot. But he'd been eight by the time of his father's crime. Eight years to embed his father's twisted thinking. Who knew what that had done to his own psyche? What sort of father *he'd* be?

'I…' Cora shook her head. 'I don't know what to say.'

To his amazement, instead of keeping her distance, she stepped closer, taking his hand in hers, threading their fingers together.

Strato's breath snagged in astonishment. He still recalled the weeks after the fire, the number of people who'd watched him with repugnance or fascination, as if he wore the visible taint of his father's crime. The only exceptions had been the professionals who were paid to be kind, and his aunt.

Cora squeezed his hand and warmth flooded from his hand up his arm. His skin tingled. He couldn't tell if it was pain as if frozen muscles thawed or something else.

He should step away but couldn't. He looked into her grave eyes and couldn't tear his attention away.

'I'm so glad you survived. Though I can't imagine how tough it's been.' Her voice resonated with feeling and Strato found himself wanting to reassure her that it was okay. But things weren't okay and he couldn't raise her hopes that his story had a happy ending.

'How *did* you get away? Or don't you want to talk about it?'

What did it matter? He'd been haunted by memories since the paternity test results. Besides, she was the first person he'd spoken to about this in over two decades and he wanted her to understand.

'I was sick that day with a stomach upset. I hadn't been able to keep down food and I was resting in bed. I woke to noise, but I couldn't make out what it was. Then it all went quiet and my father came to the room, bringing hot milk to help me sleep.'

Strato had been stunned. His father wasn't supposed to be there and he'd never before brought a bedtime drink. But Strato knew better than to ask questions of his father so he'd obediently sipped the sweetened milk.

'He'd drugged the milk.' Strato swallowed hard. 'But it made me feel sick, so after he went out I tipped it out the window.' He'd been terrified his father would find out. 'I waited for my mother to come and say goodnight but she didn't.' He felt his jaw clench.

'Strato. You don't have to tell me. I'm sorry I asked.' Cora held his hand with both hers now, stroking and comforting.

He curled his fingers around hers. Her touch, and her understanding, felt so good.

'There's not much more. Eventually I heard noises and noticed a funny, sharp smell. When I saw smoke coming under the door I tried to get out but it was locked, so I pushed out the screen on my window and got out that way.' It sounded simple, but every moment had been fraught with fear and confusion. At eight he hadn't known what was happening or what he should do.

'When I got outside I saw the fire. I tried to get in another window to help Melissa and Alex, and my mother, but couldn't get it open. So I turned to go next door for help but there was an explosion. The next thing I remember was being in a hospital bed.' He'd been frantic about his family and for a long time no one would tell him what had happened. That dreadful limbo had felt like an extension of the nightmare.

'That's where you got the scar.'

Strato blinked and focused on Cora. 'Sorry?'

'The scar on your shoulder. It looks like a burn.'

'Yes, it's a memento of that night.'

'Oh, Strato!' Cora released his hand and stepped in, wrapping her arms around him. Her hair tickled his chin as she pressed close and more of that delicious warmth seeped into his rigid body. Oh, he could get used to this.

That was half the problem. He already was.

Even knowing he did the right thing, deciding to break with Cora, it was a struggle. Part of him wanted to forget about being responsible and grab her close.

Grab everything she offered and more. As if this one remarkable woman could turn his life around.

He closed his eyes and let his arms fold around her, lightly at first, then strongly, hauling her hard against him in a convulsive movement.

He wanted her. So badly. Wanted the joy and light she'd brought him. The sincerity and honesty.

Had his father ever felt like this? Had he craved happiness and been unable to resist the allure of that one, special woman? Had he known the damage he'd do, yet been unable to resist?

Firm hands cupped the back of his head, pushing through his hair and pulling him down. Her lips, soft and intoxicating, whispered against his and the ache in his chest burst into a fiery blast of longing. Of need so deep it channelled through his bones.

Strato teetered on the brink of giving in. He *needed* to give in, for the force of his yearning was stronger than any temptation he'd felt in his life.

His lips opened, brushing hers and he drew in the taste of her, sweet and alluring. Peace beckoned. He bent closer.

Abruptly realisation slammed into him.

He was taking. No matter that Cora offered. That was what the men in his family did. They took and took. They demanded. And when they couldn't have everything exactly the way they wanted…

His fingers clamped on Cora's arms. For a second longer he lost himself in the glory of her kiss. Then he stepped back, holding her at arm's length and looking down into drowned golden-brown eyes full of compassion.

Strato locked his jaw.

He didn't want her compassion.

He wanted *everything*.

Which was why he couldn't allow himself to have anything.

'Cora. No. I can't.'

Her eyes narrowed as if she looked deep into his soul. 'But you want to.' She said it as if it were a revelation.

'Of course I want to. I haven't stopped wanting you for a second! Even when I thought, hoped, you lied about being pregnant, I still craved you.'

He'd said too much. Strato saw that in the flare of emotion in her expression.

He released her and stepped back even further, making it clear there'd be no more physical contact. Though he yearned for it with a ferocity that astounded him.

Proof that he could easily become obsessive about her? He hated to think it. He'd told himself for years that he wasn't like his old man. Yet he couldn't take the risk.

Especially now she carried his child.

Strato had spent most of his life denying he wanted a family. It was a shock to learn how wrong he'd been. How the new life Cora carried made him think, not only of his monstrous father, but of his beloved mother and his siblings. Of the times the four of them had been happy. Of the bond they'd shared and how he still missed them.

Why had he escaped when they hadn't?

'Strato?' He realised his gaze had dropped to Cora's abdomen where she cradled his child.

'Sorry?'

'I still want you too.' Her smile was an endearingly crooked line.

It was more than he'd let himself hope, after the way he'd treated her. 'I don't deserve you, *Coritsa*.'

The terrible thing was that, even now, he was tempted to do something irresponsible and dangerous, like pretend he was an ordinary guy, and persuade her to stay with him.

'You see now why I can't be a father. Our child deserves better.'

So did she.

'You can't—'

'I can and I will.' He forced his shoulders back, standing straight and shoving his hands into his pockets. 'Don't you see, I can't afford to take the risk? Not with you or our baby.'

They meant so much to him. More than he'd dreamed possible. Imagine how possessive of them he'd grow as time progressed. He had to cut these ties before they twisted into something ugly.

Slowly Cora shook her head. 'You're not that sort of man.'

'Aren't I? How do you know?'

'I know something about you, Strato. It wasn't just sex we shared, remember?' A flash of temper warmed her gaze and he felt it as a delicious shiver down his spine. He'd give everything to bask in that freely. 'I know a lot about you. Enough to know you're not cruel or—'

'Manipulative? Have you forgotten how I coerced you into being my lover? How I used your concern for your father for my own ends?'

'I haven't forgotten, Strato. But I had a choice. I could have said no. You didn't force me.'

His mouth tightened. How had he forgotten her obstinacy?

'It doesn't concern you that I'm possessive?'

'You are?' Instead of looking worried Cora's face brightened.

Strato frowned. 'I spent all that evening in Athens fuming whenever another man tried to flirt with you. I hated the way they salivated over you in that red dress. I wanted to shove them all away, or, better yet, take you somewhere private where only I could admire you.'

'I like that you didn't want to share me with other men.'

'Don't you see? That's not a good thing. Jealousy is a curse. It's a step on the way to obsession.'

The trait of his father's he most feared. The man had been a control freak, seeing his wife and children as extensions of himself. They were supposed to do what he said at all times.

Cora shook her head. 'Not necessarily. I felt jealous of those women eating you up with their eyes. And *I'm* not obsessive.'

'What women?'

She made an impatient sound. 'The women at the dinner in Athens. I'm sure some of them would have gone with you if you'd invited them.' She looked away then darted a sideways glance at him. 'Then there are all those other women you've been with. I don't like them. Any of them.'

Astonished, Strato rocked back on his heels.

Cora sounded jealous.

Where had that come from?

'*I think* the fact you didn't like other men looking at me is positive. It means you feel the connection between us too.' Now she looked him straight in the eye, chin up and hands on her hips. The sight made something in his chest roll over. He liked her feistiness, her determination.

Liked? There was an understatement. He felt too much for this woman. The temptation to ignore the risk and pursue what sounded like an invitation was too alluring. He had to end this, now.

'I'm sorry, Cora, but it can't be. Ever. I know where feelings like that could lead me.' Because his father's taint loomed like a shadow. Strato's next breath felt like a blade slicing his lungs. 'I experienced it. You didn't. I refuse to take a chance of something like that happening to you or our child.'

The fire in her eyes dimmed. Her pugnacious attitude softened. 'Oh, Strato, you—'

'My lawyers will be in touch about a settlement.' He turned away, knowing he had to go before he reached for her again.

'Wait!'

He paused, but didn't turn back.

'Please, give me one more day before you leave. There may be things we need to discuss. Things I'd prefer to talk with you about, not a lawyer.'

Strato narrowed his eyes against the glitter of sunlight on the sea. But it wasn't the view he saw, it was Cora. She filled his mind, his soul, even the heart he'd tried to tell himself he no longer possessed.

'Very well. I'll stay another twenty-four hours.' But he prayed, with a fervour he hadn't felt for decades, that Cora would see sense and not drag this out. Better that he leave and never look back.

CHAPTER FIFTEEN

CORA'S LITTLE BOAT puttered out in the early morning light. As it drew in close it was completely dwarfed by the magnificent lines of Strato's luxurious yacht. Cora didn't care. She was well past being intimidated by his wealth.

Strato was just a man, as flawed as any other, even if he was also magnificent.

Her heart squeezed as she thought of him yesterday, doing what he believed to be the right thing by their unborn child, looking all the while like a man on the edge. His fortune was no protection against unhappiness or the terrible burden he carried.

The story of his past had undone her. What must he have suffered? It put his determination to remain unattached in a different light. His voice when he'd mentioned the family he'd lost…

It was obvious his guilt over surviving when they didn't was real and raw.

So here she was, gambling her future on the slim chance Strato felt more than protectiveness for her and the baby. Hoping he felt even a little of what she did.

For what she'd learned yesterday had made her bruised heart open even further. She'd loved Strato when he was strong and sexy, when she felt cherished and sheltered in his arms. But her feelings were even stronger now, knowing how much he'd suffered, how much he'd missed out on and still did. How he thought not of himself but of her and their baby.

How could any woman who cared turn her back on him, having heard the truth?

The odds were against her. He was so fiercely determined to protect her and their child from himself. All she had on her side was his admission that he still wanted her. And the strength of her feelings.

So she'd taken her time to work out her strategy. It didn't amount to much, a few arguments she hoped might convince him, and her sexy red dress that had distracted him in Athens.

Strato was no fool, he'd realise she'd dressed up for a reason, but she'd use whatever tools she had.

As she neared the yacht Manoli, Strato's assistant, waved and took the line Cora tossed him, securing it.

'It's good to see you, Cora.' He lowered his voice as he held out his hand to help her aboard. 'I'm worried about him.'

She nodded. 'So am I.' Distress over Strato's story, and the slim chances of making him see sense, had kept her awake most of the night. He couldn't go on like that, cutting himself off from everyone, believing he was evil incarnate when he, more than anyone, was a victim. 'Where is he?'

'In his study, though he seems to be brooding more than working.'

'I'll see myself in if that's okay.'

'Great idea. If you don't improve his mood, nothing

will.' Manoli's sweeping glance and appreciative smile boosted her confidence.

Her dress was the sexiest thing she'd ever worn and she'd spent ages washing then brushing her hair till it shone. She'd even put on enough make-up to give her eyes a smoky look and emphasise the shape of her lips. She wore a delicate chain necklace in the shape of a bow with long tails that fell low and drew the eye to her cleavage.

Yet her stomach was full of butterflies as she pushed open the door to Strato's study. His back was to her as he stared out to sea. For a second she had leisure to take him in, broad straight shoulders beneath a white shirt and pale trousers pulled tight over his perfect rear by the hands shoved in his front pockets.

'Strato.'

He spun towards her and for a fleeting moment she read welcome in his expression, before a scowl descended. 'I'd hoped you'd make this easy for both of us, Cora.'

She stepped into the room, shutting the door behind her. 'You promised you'd hear me out if there were things we need to discuss.'

'Well?' His look, his stance were pure arrogant billionaire. As if she took up too much of his precious time. But Cora wasn't fooled. This man felt deeply, too deeply, and he cared, even if he tried to give the impression he didn't.

'I have a proposition, Strato. I want you to live with me, not as a temporary lover, but as my partner.'

His eyebrows shot up and his eyes widened. 'Didn't you hear *anything* I said yesterday? I can't live with you, what if I...?'

'And what if you don't, Strato? You're denying us all, you, me and our baby, the chance of happiness, because you're afraid of something that's not going to happen.'

He stepped closer then stopped abruptly as if fearing to get too close. 'You ask me to forget the danger to you both? I can't do that.'

Cora folded her arms and saw with a flicker of hope the way his gaze followed the movement, lingering a fraction on her breasts.

'You're making assumptions, Strato, and any scientist will tell you that's unwise. You're acting without proof.'

He shook his head. 'The proof being an act of violence? I refuse to risk it.'

'Don't you see, your thinking is flawed? I understand your fear about learning behaviour patterns from your father and grandfather. But have you stopped to consider that the very fact you refuse to take this chance points to you being different?'

'You haven't known me long enough to form an opinion, Cora.' His dismissive tone might have stopped her once. Now she saw it as camouflage for his pain and doubt.

She paced closer, glad she'd taken time to pull together her information and marshal her arguments.

'I did some research yesterday, Strato. There are plenty of press reports about you but not one mentioning violence or abuse of women.' He opened his mouth but she kept speaking. 'I also rang Steph Nicolaides, who spoke to her husband.'

'You did what?' He looked stunned.

'Don't worry, I didn't share your past. I told her how

I felt about you and asked if she was aware of anything I should know about you.'

Not because Cora doubted him for a second. But so Strato could hear what others thought of him. He respected Damen and trusted his acumen. She hoped Damen's feedback would make Strato stop and think instead of instinctively rejecting what others saw and he couldn't.

'How do you feel about me?'

His eyes bored into hers. Cora swallowed and reminded herself this was no time for pride.

'I love you.'

Strato moved towards her then stopped abruptly.

'You can't!'

He was breathless, his voice cracking, and all the feelings she battled to contain surfaced. She wanted to hold him and comfort him. Rock him in her arms, take him into her body and whisper soothing words to erase his pain. She wanted to take those lovely, wide shoulders and shake him!

'I can and I do.' When he would have spoken, she raised her palm. 'You can't control my feelings, Strato. I've loved you since well before I learned about our baby. My feelings are true and real and I wouldn't change them if I could.'

She watched him reach for his desk as if he needed support. Good. Maybe a few shocks would knock some sense into him.

'Steph said you were kind and generous and that you'd make a terrific father if you could be persuaded to settle down.' Seeing Strato's shock, Cora hurried on. 'Not that she knows about the baby. She said Damen thinks highly of you and trusts you. He said you're a truly decent man, masquerading as someone who doesn't care.'

Cora agreed.

Strato's mouth twisted in a jeering smile. 'Much as I appreciate the praise, none of that counters my concerns.'

'What about Asteri?'

He stiffened. 'Asteri?'

'Don't look so surprised. I know you're associated with it, even if you don't run it. I told you I'd been digging.'

Strato's lowered brows told her he wasn't happy.

'Where did the name come from? Since it means *star*, it made me think of a bright light to guide you in tough times. Is that it? It's appropriate for an organisation that gives on-the-ground support to victims of family violence.'

'You *have* done your homework.' He didn't sound pleased.

'I kept seeing hotel bookings from Asteri, for single women or sometimes for women with children. I got curious.' She'd found a charity that provided safe housing and services to families affected by violence. 'Those holidays you've paid for aren't just for employees. Some are for survivors of trauma.'

'I don't see the relevance.'

He was *so* stubborn. 'Do you really think a man who sees women as possessions to be controlled would champion that cause? Not with a tax-deductible payment, but with a meaningful contribution like holidays they wouldn't usually be able to afford? A break when they most need it?'

Cora closed the gap between them and put her palm

to his chest, pushing. A tremor ran up her arm and encircled her chest at the thrill of touching him again.

'Don't, Cora.'

'Or what? What will you do?'

His hand closed on hers and he gently pulled it away. Yet he kept hold of it. Was it imagination that turned his touch into a caress? His grim stare into one of longing?

'Would you beat me or—?'

'Don't, Cora! This isn't a game.'

His pain created an ache that ripped through her own chest. Cora lifted her other palm to his face, cupping his jaw, feeling the roughened texture of his unshaved skin.

'I know. But you're not like your father. I look at this scientifically, look at the facts, and draw sensible conclusions.'

She didn't mention the very unscientific fact that she also followed her heart. Her instinct that Strato was the man she believed him.

'You're not violent, Strato. On the contrary, you help victims of violence.' And went to considerable trouble to do it quietly so that the public wasn't aware of his interest. 'You're incredibly protective, of me and our baby. I admire you. I care for you. I *love* you, and I want you to take a chance on turning your life around and being with me.'

She had no idea what she did.

Asking the impossible. While at the same time holding out shining hope.

Strato had never let himself think of being loved again. He knew how precious it was. Still remembered the warmth of his mother's love and his siblings'. He'd spent his life locking away what was left of his broken heart. Now Cora strode into his life, smashing barriers he'd thought impenetrable, and said she loved him. She trusted him. She wanted a future with him.

A great shudder racked him from head to toe. He tried to move back, find space to think, but couldn't bring himself to release her.

The tender touch of her palm on his face was every hope, every dream he'd tried not to harbour.

But it seemed dreams weren't so easily killed. Beneath his adamantine control something welled, hot and strong. A yearning. A need. A sense of inevitability.

Because he loved her.

Cora had worked a miracle, awakening feelings he'd never thought to experience. That was what he'd fought against recognising all these weeks.

He loved Cora with every part of his shadowed soul. With every breath he took and would ever take.

Not just because she offered the elusive promise of a future to a man who'd never allowed himself to think long term.

But because of Cora. She was everything he needed. Sensible. Sexy. Giving. Funny. Determined. Frustratingly determined.

'Strato?'

Eyes the colour of cognac held his and he felt himself on the brink of falling. He wanted to fall. To trust she was right and all would be well.

But it wouldn't be him paying the price if this ended in disaster.

'I…care for you, Cora. That's why I can't do what you want.'

He stepped away, far enough that she couldn't touch

him. She didn't follow. She looked winded, as if his rejection had undone her.

Strato wanted to tug her into his arms and tell her it would be all right. But she was too precious.

'What would your mother say, Strato?'

His head jerked back as if she'd slapped him.

'Don't bring my mother into this!'

He still grieved for her. For the fact he hadn't been able to save her.

'Would she want to see her boy turning his back on happiness? Wouldn't she want to see you with your own family, feeling joy and tenderness? Do you think she'd be happy seeing you pursuing meaningless hook-ups that diminish you instead of sustaining you?'

How had Cora known? That was exactly how it felt. He'd realised in the time they'd been apart that he could never go back to those brief sexual encounters.

Because what he wanted was Cora. For ever.

His nemesis continued. 'I suspect she'd hope that, despite what happened to your family, you'd find true peace and happiness. That you'd love.'

Strato drew a slow breath and released it.

Cora was right. His mother had been positive, despite her abusive marriage. She'd told him to reach for the sky and dream big. That was why the charity he'd established was called Asteri. That and the fact she'd always called him *asteri mou*, my star.

'You're right.' The words ground from his constricted throat. 'But I can't seek happiness at your expense.'

The dawning light in Cora's eyes dimmed as her mouth thinned. She planted her hands on her generous hips, drawing his unwilling attention to the marvellous curve at her trim waist and up to those magnificent breasts.

'You don't think I have the strength to stand up for myself, Strato?' Her chest heaved and he looked up, discovering her eyes narrowed in anger. 'Well, I can.' She paused and he wondered what argument she'd try next.

She dropped her arms and breathed slowly, as if through pain.

Had he convinced her? Why didn't he feel pleased? He knew an unreasoning urge to bar the door to stop her going.

'If that's your final word, there's nothing left to say.' Her gaze held his and he read distress there that matched his own, making him even more miserable. 'But know this, Strato Doukas. I want my baby to have two loving parents like I did. It may take a while, years even, but I'll find a man who's not afraid of commitment. A man who'll truly care for me and help me raise my child.'

Unbelievable pain filled Strato's chest, clogging the space behind his ribs till he couldn't breathe.

'You wouldn't.' The thought of Cora with another man, a stranger raising his child...

'Why not? I'm not going to live like a hermit because you don't want me.' She looked away. 'You might have broken my heart.' She paused, swallowing, and his own heart shattered. 'But thanks to you, I've discovered I like sex. There are decent men out there who could be a father to this baby. It mightn't be a love match but, as you've also taught me, love doesn't guarantee a happy ending.'

'You're bluffing!' She had to be.

Cora turned towards the door, the hem of her skirt flaring, teasing him with a glimpse of toned thighs.

'Someone like Manoli maybe. I like his sense of humour. And he's got infinite patience. He has to have, working for you—'

Strato's hand on her arm stopped her mid-step.

Go to Manoli indeed! When she professed to love *him*.

Cora swung around and he couldn't help himself. Fear and desperation melded into an unstoppable force. He hauled her close and put his mouth on hers, the threads of his control finally tearing.

Firm hands captured his head, holding tight as if she feared he'd pull back. All that wonderful womanly softness pressed against him, splintering any thought of self-control. And her kiss…

Strato sighed. She kissed like a woman in love. As desperate as he.

He wrapped his arms securely around her and gave himself up to the inevitable. Amazingly, it didn't feel like defeat, but victory, optimism.

It was a long time before he could summon enough control to lift his head and find his voice.

'Witch.' Even to his own ears the growl sounded like an endearment. 'You had no intention of pursuing Manoli or anyone else, had you?'

'You expected me to fight fair when our happiness is at stake? Our whole future and our child's?' Her eyes shone overbright. 'Kiss me again, Strato. Please?'

Her wobbly voice undid him. It matched his own shuddering wonder.

How could he refuse her? Even knowing she'd played him, had him dancing to her tune. She'd broken him down to his most elemental being and reassembled him so he felt trembling belief in the possibility of a future.

He just couldn't relinquish it, or her. Not now.

Finally, it seemed hours later, he sat with her bundled on his lap, warm and luscious in his arms. Strato inhaled the scent of wild honey as he nuzzled her neck and knew that whatever the future held, *this* was right. She was right for him.

'I love you, Cora.' It felt amazing to say it aloud.

She turned, eyes shining with wonder.

Strato swallowed, pushing down fear and clutching at hope. The precious gift Cora brought him.

'Oh, Strato!' Her eyes brimmed with tears, but she smiled through them and the sight of her joy gave him hope for the future.

'I want to make you happy, always. But I don't know how.'

She shook her head. 'For a clever man you have a lot to learn. Just keep on being you and I'll be happy.'

'That I can do. I just wish—'

Her finger on his lips stopped him. 'How about we promise to take it a day at a time? You're not the only one who has to learn about building a future together. And being a parent.'

Strato lifted her hand to his lips. 'But we're in this together.' The power of that thought sustained him against the shadows of fear. He'd do everything he could to build a wonderful future for them all. There was no other possible alternative. 'You and me together, *Coritsa*. We'll make mistakes but we'll learn. If I have your love that's all I need.'

Cora's tender smile eased a little of his ancient hurts. Who knew what a lifetime of them together could achieve?

'You have it, *agapi mou*. Always.'

EPILOGUE

'LOOK, DADDY, LOOK!' Melissa turned her gap-toothed grin and bright eyes on Strato and he felt that familiar hit of joy. 'There's another. Isn't it cute?'

She pointed to the tiny, just-hatched turtle, crawling across the sand towards the sea.

'Absolutely,' he murmured. 'Almost as cute as you.'

She giggled and threw herself at his legs, hugging hard. 'I love you, Daddy.'

As ever, those words made his heart turn over. Even though he was now part of a family that spoke openly about such emotion.

'And I love you, my little princess.' He scooped her up in his arms, whirling her high till she giggled.

'Shh! You'll scare them,' Alex cautioned. Strato turned to see his son at the water's edge with his grandfather and Doris. Serious, warm-hearted Alex and carefree Melissa. The twins lit up Strato's world, as their namesakes, his siblings, had years before.

'We promise to be quiet. Don't we?' Melissa nodded and he put her down, watching her skip off to the others.

This was a regular outing. All the family came to Cora's island when it was time for the hatchlings to appear. Strato had built a house on the main island across the headland from his father-in-law's hotel and this was just a short boat ride away.

'Thank you, *agapi mou*.' An arm slipped around his waist and there was Cora, his wife, his love, his life. He pulled her satisfyingly close, his smile widening.

'What for? The island?' He'd bought it in her name, as part of a successful proposal to turn the area into a marine park. Now it was protected from development and a new research facility did important work, also providing opportunities for researchers like his wife.

Glowing golden-brown eyes met his and desire stirred. 'That too. And for inviting Steph, Damen and the kids to visit next week for our anniversary party.' She paused, her mouth curling in a tender smile. 'But mainly thank you for believing in us. For trusting yourself, and me. I love you, Strato. I can't tell you how much.'

Her misty eyes and sweet smile told him. As did the ache of pure joy that filled him.

'As much as I love you, *Coritsa*.' His love for her filled him to the brim and always would. 'I give thanks every day that we found each other.'

She'd saved him from himself and taught him how to live in the sunlight instead of the shadows. He leant in and, here at the place where they'd met, Strato kissed his own, special Nereid with all the love in his heart.

* * * * *

If you lost yourself in
A Consequence Made in Greece, *why not have a look
at these other Annie West stories?*

Contracted to Her Greek Enemy
Claiming His Out-of-Bounds Bride
The King's Bride by Arrangement
The Sheikh's Marriage Proclamation
Pregnant with His Majesty's Heir

Available now!

WE HOPE YOU ENJOYED
THIS BOOK FROM

◈ HARLEQUIN
PRESENTS

Escape to exotic locations where passion knows no bounds.

Welcome to the glamorous lives of royals and billionaires,
where passion knows no bounds. Be swept into a world
of luxury, wealth and exotic locations.

8 NEW BOOKS AVAILABLE EVERY MONTH!

HPHALO2021

#3945 HER BEST KEPT ROYAL SECRET
Heirs for Royal Brothers
by Lynne Graham

Independent Gaby thought nothing could be more life-changing than waking up in the bed of the playboy prince who was so dangerous to her heart... Until she's standing in front of Angel a year later, sharing her shocking secret—his son!

#3946 CROWNED FOR HIS DESERT TWINS
by Clare Connelly

To become king, Sheikh Khalil must marry...immediately. But first, a mind-blowing whirlwind night with India McCarthy that neither can resist! When India reveals she's pregnant, can a ring secure his crown...and his heirs?

#3947 FORBIDDEN TO HER SPANISH BOSS
The Acostas!
by Susan Stephens

Rose Kelly can't afford any distractions. Especially her devilishly attractive boss, Raffa Acosta! But a week of networking on his superyacht may take them from professional to dangerously passionate territory...

#3948 SHY INNOCENT IN THE SPOTLIGHT
The Scandalous Campbell Sisters
by Melanie Milburne

Elspeth's sheltered existence means she's hesitant to swap places with her exuberant twin for a glamorous wedding. But the social spotlight is nothing compared to the laser focus of cynical billionaire Mack's undivided attention...

#3949 PROOF OF THEIR ONE HOT NIGHT
The Infamous Cabrera Brothers
by Emmy Grayson

One soul-stirring night with notorious tycoon Alejandro leaves Calandra pregnant. She plans to raise the baby alone. He's determined to prove he's parent material—and tempt her into another smoldering encounter...

#3950 HOW TO TEMPT THE OFF-LIMITS BILLIONAIRE
South Africa's Scandalous Billionaires
by Joss Wood

On a mission to acquire Roisin's South African vineyard, tycoon Muzi knows he needs to keep his eyes on the business deal, not his best friend's sister. Only, their forbidden temptation leads to even more forbidden nights...

#3951 THE ITALIAN'S BRIDE ON PAPER
by Kim Lawrence

When arrogant billionaire Samuele arrives at her door announcing his claim to her nephew, he sends Maya's senses into overdrive... She refuses to leave the baby's side, so he demands more—her as his convenient wife!

#3952 REDEEMED BY HIS NEW YORK CINDERELLA
by Jadesola James

Kitty will do anything for the foundation inspired by her tumultuous childhood. Even agree to a fake relationship to help Laurence, the impossibly guarded man from her past, land his next deal. Only, their chemistry is anything but make-believe!

YOU CAN FIND MORE INFORMATION ON UPCOMING HARLEQUIN TITLES, FREE EXCERPTS AND MORE AT HARLEQUIN.COM.

HPCNMRB0921